I GET TO LOVE YOU

Texas Roots Book 1

Charity Christy

This is a work of fiction. Names, characters, places, and incidents are a product of the author's imagination. Locales and public names are sometimes used for atmospheric purposes. Any resemblance to actual people, living or dead, or to businesses, companies, events, institutions, or locales is completely coincidental.

Book Layout © 2017 BookDesignTemplates.com

Book Cover © 2017 Victorine Lieske

Author Photo © 2016 Lauren Elizabeth Powel

I Get to Love You/ Charity Christy
ISBN: 978-0692896044
ISBN-10: 069289604X

Books By This Author

Texas Roots

I Get to Love You – Melissa & Blake

To Believe in You – Aly & Colt

Jade & Luke (COMING SOON)

Cami & James (COMING SOON)

From the Author

Dear Reader,

I want to first say thank you for reading *I Get to Love You*. It has always been a dream of mine to write books and this is my very first one! It has been a life changing journey for me. You'll learn so much about yourself when you spend an unbelievable amount of time alone in your own head. I feel like I've grown as a writer and person because of this experience.

I Get to Love You is a contemporary inspirational clean romance. It evolved from a vision that I had of a girl walking through sunflowers and became a story of forgiveness and love. I have fallen in love with Blake and Melissa. I've spent countless hours with them, individually and together, and feel like they are a part of my family. I wrote this book to help inspire men and women everywhere to see that they can move beyond the dark shadows of their past. Our past doesn't have to control how we see our future. With renewed faith, God can help us forgive and love in the deepest way possible.

If you enjoyed this book, please leave a review at Amazon and Goodreads. Reviews are a major asset to authors and help allow them to continue to write more stories.

I'd love to get to know you! Visit my blog at www.charitychristy.com. You can also find me on Facebook, Twitter, Instagram, and Pinterest.

XO

Charity

CONTENTS

Prologue

A cool breeze from the north swept through the field making the sunflowers dance in the wind. The golden sunset radiated off the flowers' golden faces. Melissa Adair sighed at the relief the wind brought from the hot Texas heat. Just like the sunflowers, the pages of her notebook waved with the wind. Her grandparents' sunflower field had always been a place where Melissa felt most comfortable, secure, and at peace. The sunflowers opened up where a giant oak tree stood in front of a pond. This was her favorite spot in the world. It was the place she came when she was her happiest and also when she was at her darkest. Just her, nature, a pen, and paper. In this very spot, Melissa poured her heart out on paper and in prayer. She dealt with every emotion that a teenage girl could possibly go through.

She leaned her head back against the sturdy oak and closed her eyes, drawing stability from its trunk. She took a deep breath and exhaled slowly. It was August and summer was coming to an end. All the change fixing to take place caused her shoulders to drop slightly by the weight. This summer had been perfect and in a way, she didn't want it to end, even though the end meant another beginning.

"Mind if I join you?"

A smile spread across her face at the sound of her favorite voice in the world. *Blake.* Without even opening her eyes, she patted at the worn spot next to her saved only for him. The grass gave as he settled in next to her. She slid her arm under his and laced their fingers together. Closing her notebook, she laid it on the grass next to her.

"Did you write anything good?" Blake's voice was light and she could hear the smile behind his words.

"Probably not."

He squeezed her hand. "Of course it is. You're going to be a big-time writer before you know it."

She loved how confident he was about her. No matter how unsure she was about things, Blake held her up to believe the best in herself. No one would ever know how amazing that was considering his home life. He kept his demons hidden from most everyone.

Blake Knoll was her best friend, with the exception of Jade and her cousin, Aly. But this friendship was different than the girls. Blake was the first boy she ever considered her best friend, but it was more than that. He was her first love. They both had dealt with things at home, his worse than hers, but they found support in each other.

Their friendship was unlikely. He was a star baseball player and ran with the popular kids. Everyone wanted to be his friend. Blake had a talent that gave him confidence and he was well liked because of it. Melissa didn't feel like she stood out. It was easy for her to blend into the background. Sometimes she felt the only real reason he ever noticed her was because he lived across the street. Earlier that year, her father ran out on her and her mom, forcing them to move in with her grandparents. It became apparent that Blake didn't have the glamorous life of a popular jock behind closed doors. His home life was quite the opposite.

Any time Melissa would see Mr. Knoll he was staggering around and yelling about something. Mrs. Knoll was very thin and silently went along with all of it. There had been a few times where they got into fights outside and Melissa saw them. Then she noticed Mr. Knoll yelling at Blake once and tried to swing at him. Blake ducked and Mr. Knoll fell to the ground. Despite this, Blake always had a smile on his face and a positive attitude at school.

One night Melissa was headed out to walk through the sunflowers when she spotted Blake sitting on the tailgate of his truck. He was dabbing a wet cloth on his lip and when he looked up she could see it was busted. It broke her heart to see him so drained of happiness. She walked over to him and asked if he wanted to take a walk. To her surprise he actually said yes. From that moment on they developed a friendship of support, which blossomed into her first love.

The very spot they were resting in, had become their sanctuary, together.

"Penny for 'em," Blake's voice cut through her memories.

She turned to look up at him and found his sea blue eyes smiling back at her. She returned his smile. "Oh, just thinking about everything."

"Like what?"

She glanced back toward the pond. "I just can't believe how much my life has changed the past two years. I've been so happy." Her eyes dropped down to their intertwined fingers. "And I can't believe it's all changing tomorrow."

Blake brought her fingers to his lips and kissed them lightly. "Everything's going to be ok."

"How do you know that?" she asked looking up at him.

His eyes never wavered from hers. "Faith. I believe that the best is still ahead of us. I know it sounds like a song on the radio but it's true. You're moving to college next week and…"

"You're leaving for basic tomorrow," she interrupted.

Her words made his shoulders drop but his eyes never left hers. "I'm not saying it's not going to be hard but I'm going to make a promise to you."

"What's that?"

"I know we'll be separated and I'm not sure what will happen after basic, that's almost 4 months from now. You're going to be finishing up your first semester and getting ready for finals. I know there are unknowns and it's a lot to think about, but I promise that I will come back for you. I don't know when that'll be, but if you wait I'll come back."

She closed her eyes and dropped her head unable to look at him. Her heart believed him and trusted that he meant every word he was saying. She supported him when he told her he wanted to enlist.

But now that they were sitting in their spot for what would be the last time in their foreseeable future, her heart was breaking.

He must have noticed the build of emotion because he got on his knees in front of her. She didn't know if she could look at him.

"Melissa," Blake's voice was soft. When she didn't raise her head, he gently pressed his forehead to hers. "I'll come back for you. Do you believe me?"

"Yes." Her voice was shaky. She did believe he meant it and she prayed it would come true.

"I love you." He wiped the tears that had escaped her eyes with his thumbs. Then he leaned in and kissed her.

"I love you, too." She meant it with all her heart. Melissa pulled out an old pocket watch and flipped it open. "I want to show you something."

"Ok," Blake said looking at the watch.

"It's a pocket watch Gram gave me. It used to belong to my Pops." She turned the watch to show him the picture inside. "This picture is of them before they got married. I want to add a picture of us underneath theirs."

She popped out her grandparents' picture and pushed a picture of her and Blake sitting in that very spot into the backing. Then she returned the original picture on top. "The watch doesn't work anymore but I like that. When that picture was taken, their love was frozen in time. Nothing can change the love they shared because it's captured forever. I want us to be like that too." She closed the watch and looked up at him. "I want to keep this here in our spot. There's a notch above us that I want to hide it in. So, when the day comes that we return to this spot, no matter what has happened, we're reminded of what we have."

"I can't wait." Blake kissed her forehead and breathed her in, realizing he didn't know when he'd see her next.

She'd be lying if she said she wasn't worried about the obstacles that would likely challenge Blake's promise. He settled back next to her and she rested her head on his shoulder. But for their last few hours she pushed those thoughts out of her mind and just enjoyed the feel of him next to her. She would keep the faith and believe that Blake was right. Their best days were ahead of them no matter what trial they had to go through to get there.

Chapter 1

Eight Years Later

Turning back toward her cup of tea, Melissa took a drink and let it wash over her insides like a warm bath. Not even the Texas heat could change her love of hot tea. She also loved this little coffee shop. It was the only one in Shaw Creek and she'd been going there since high school. The small town was really a suburb south of Dallas, but with the interstate on the outskirts of town, it felt a lot smaller than a typical suburb. Though not a coffee drinker herself, she loved the atmosphere. The smell of fresh coffee grounds, the light conversations amongst customers, and the rustic charm made Melissa feel inspired. It was the perfect place to write, both personal pieces and articles for the Shaw Creek Daily Press.

One of the perks of being a teacher was the free summer months, when Melissa was able to partake in her other love: writing. Journalism was Melissa's first love and the dream job she had always wanted. But she loved teaching more than she thought she would. It was the perfect job for a single mom and she hadn't anticipated how much she would enjoy the kids. But now was not the time to pull out her laptop or notes because her older sister, Cami, would arrive any minute. Melissa pulled out her phone to check the time. Of course, Cami was running late. Melissa was always waiting on her sister, no matter the occasion.

"Melissa, sorry I'm late," Cami slid into the chair across from Melissa and dumped her bag on the floor.

"It's alright," Melissa smiled at her older sister.

Cami's blonde hair was thrown up into a messy bun and her pink scrubs were hard to miss. No matter if Cami just walked out of the salon or was coming off a twelve-hour shift, she always looked amazing. Melissa could spend an hour getting ready and still not be able to pull off Cami's look.

Cami pulled out a folder of papers. "I wanted to get your opinion on…" She paused and looked up. "Where's that sweet nephew of mine?"

"Wyatt's at the summer youth program at the city library today."

Cami sat back. "Oh. Aren't you supposed to be there too? Did I make you have to leave?"

"No. I'm starting next week with the reading and writing tutoring. It's like summer school, but more fun for the kids. I'll pick him up in a few hours."

"You're such a good mommy. Wyatt is so lucky to have you," Cami said with a smile.

"Thanks. I sure try." Melissa ran her finger along the rim of her tea cup.

"I mean it, Mel. Being a single mother after what you went through and what you lost as a result is amazing. You're a great teacher, you volunteer with different programs, and you give so much to your son. Don't sell yourself short, ok?"

Cami's words struck a chord with Melissa. Compliments were something she didn't like. Not that she didn't appreciate them, she was just uncomfortable taking them. She'd been used and tossed aside without a second thought. As a result, she doubted she was worth the compliments, the appreciation, or the love. It had been a long time since she'd felt special to anyone. She had been in love only one time in her life, when she was eighteen. He was still the only man she ever thought she would have a future with. But because of one horrible event that all changed.

Melissa closed her eyes and could see the party house, smell the alcohol, and hear the loud music. Her heart rate increased as she saw the red drink and tasted the fruity flavor. Then everything was fuzzy and the bedroom was dark. Confusion. Pressure. Pain. Melissa shook her head wishing the nightmare away as the nameless guy's face appeared in her memory.

Cami shuffled around some papers bringing Melissa back to the coffee shop. "I need your opinion on these final details for the reception hall. I want to finalize with the florist since I'm working extra hours before the wedding. I guess they're having me make up for the week I'll be missing while on our honeymoon."

Cami had been working at the Dallas Cancer Center for two years. The center was about a forty-five minute drive with morning traffic, but Cami wanted to be close to James and that was in Shaw Creek. Cami was so great at helping the patients cope with their diagnosis and treatment. Regardless of how spontaneous or high maintenance she may appear to be, Cami had a heart of gold and loved her job.

Melissa listened to Cami talk about what style she wanted for the guest tables, the back drop, the food tables and the chairs. This was not going to be a small affair, that's not how Cami did things. Even though it may not be what Melissa would picture as a perfect wedding, it was definitely perfect for Cami. Once they decided on the pinks, greens, and oranges for the arrangements, Cami moved on to the ribbons and table cloths.

"There's so much to do and I only have a few weeks outside of work to get everything finalized."

Melissa shook her head. "I know it's coming up fast. You'll get it all done."

"I hope so. I feel like I've spent all this time planning, but have procrastinated in actually bringing anything to life. Work has been rough and the days are slipping by quicker than I want them to."

It was hard to believe Cami was getting married in a little over a month. It seemed like they had been planning for years, not six months. James was perfect for Cami and they complimented each other. James was able to ground Cami, which she needed. He doted on

Cami and showered her with gifts. He knew the way right to her heart and she loved it.

Melissa smiled at her sister as Cami thumbed through a couple other pages. She was nothing like Cami when it came to planning. Melissa worked very hard to plan everything out and have a tight schedule. Multicolored sticky notes were her best friend. Cami was more sporadic and frantic in getting things done.

After they discussed the place settings and centerpieces, Cami seemed satisfied and took a big drink from the water bottle in her bag. "So, how is my baby sister doing?"

Melissa sat back in her chair and dropped her shoulders. "Oh, I'm good. I've been busy with my weekly column for the Daily Press and Wyatt's baseball games. Next week things will be even busier when I start my tutoring at the library."

"Any dating prospects in your sights?" Cami was fishing. Melissa just sighed knowing she wouldn't let it go.

"Not really. I don't think I have the time for that right now."

"Oh come on, Mel. You need to get out there and start dating again. When was the last time you actually went on a date?"

Melissa dropped her eyes to her hands. "I don't know. A few months. The last guy was that banker, Shane."

"Shane? Mel, that was over six months ago." Cami shook her head. "You can't just let life pass you by. You're twenty-six and Wyatt's seven. It's time to try to meet someone. I don't want you to be alone."

That pricked Melissa's heart more than she wanted to admit. She did get lonely, even though she told herself that it didn't matter. She had to take care of her son and worrying about herself wasn't her main priority.

"We're not alone, really. We have Gram, Mom, you, and James."

"That doesn't count. You know what I mean."

Melissa sighed. "Perhaps it's just not in the cards for me right now. I mean I have Wyatt and we're doing really good. We don't *need* to have a man in our lives."

Cami reached across the table and squeezed her arm. "Don't be like that, Melissa. You are beautiful and deserve the very best. You will find someone and when you do you won't be able to imagine your life without him. And he will love Wyatt like his own. You'll get the family you've always wanted."

Melissa nodded to her sister. She wanted to believe that. Really. But being a single mom didn't make that easy. Sure, she saw plenty of eligible men but they weren't that excited to find out about Wyatt. She couldn't imagine her life without Wyatt even if men didn't want to take on such "baggage". Melissa winced at the thought of anyone looking at Wyatt as anything other than a blessing because that is exactly what he was. Maybe she'd find someone after Wyatt was a little older.

Cami leaned back in her seat and took another drink. Melissa noticed the glimmer of light from her engagement ring. Melissa looked down at her bare left hand and wondered what it would be like to see something there one day.

"Ok, I'm moving on." Cami's words made Melissa jump. Cami took another drink and then stuffed her wedding folder back in her bag. "Thank you so much for helping. It's going to be a little crazy the next few weeks with the 4th of July and work."

"Don't stress, Cam. We'll get it done and it'll be amazing."

Cami took a deep breath and nodded. Her phone dinged and she checked it. "It's James. He's busy trying to get this project at work done. I try to help him the best I know how. I get stressed just listening to him. But I love him."

Cami beamed when she talked about James. Melissa longed to feel the same way. After the rape, she had hoped that her boyfriend at the time, Blake, might accept her and her baby. The problem was that she couldn't bring herself to risk it. If she told him she ran the risk of him *not* being ok with it. The thought of Blake rejecting her or telling her he didn't want her anymore was more than she could stand. She hadn't spoken to him since their last night in the sunflower field. She felt guilty about leaving him in the dark, but at the time it was all she could think to do.

She didn't like talking about what had happened that first semester of college, but it had brought her a blessing she didn't know she was missing. If she had to go without finding love for now it was worth it. Wyatt was worth it.

Cami lowered her phone and stood. "I have to get to work. It's a twelve-hour shift tonight." She leaned around and gave Melissa a quick side hug and said, "You're a great sister. How long are you going to stay?" She paused adjusting her purse.

"Just a little bit longer. I need to put the final touches on the next week's column. Then I have to pick Wyatt up once I leave here."

"Oh, that's right. I'll call you later."

Melissa smiled and waved as Cami headed out the front door. She leaned back in her chair and looked out the window. She watched Cami as she made her way across the street and hopped into her car. Melissa loved her sister, but with the four-year age gap she felt like Cami tended to judge the choices she made. Cami was good at giving her opinion and not worrying about how it came out. Melissa knew it was because Cami cared, but that didn't make it any easier to hear it.

She pulled out her laptop and opened next week's piece. She wanted to finish her conclusion and then send it to the newspaper. She drank the last of her now lukewarm tea, she sat back and let her fingers glide across the keys.

Chapter 2

Wisps of hair drifted across her face, as the door opened for another customer. Melissa looked up, surprised to notice the line was almost to the door. She checked her phone and realized she had about thirty minutes before she had to pick Wyatt up. She looked at her computer screen, satisfied with her article. She pulled up an email and sent it to her editor. As she shut down her computer and returned it to her bag she heard, "I'll have a Black Eye please."

The sound of the voice behind her made her heart stop. Melissa's eyes locked on the floor next to her bag, her hands froze on the zipper. It was a voice she hadn't heard in eight years but would never forget. She had often thought about this moment and what it would be like to see him again. Memories of the past sucked at her feet like quicksand, making it hard to breathe.

They were in the sunflower field sitting in their spot. The lightening bugs were dancing, their glow reflected off the pond. Her head on his shoulder. His thumb rubbing her hand. Her eyes watching the sun disappear behind the sunflowers. His cologne mixing with the smell of grass.

Everything inside Melissa was screaming to turn around and look, but she felt frozen in place. Slowly Melissa sat up in her chair and wrapped her hands around her tea cup. She didn't know if she'd ever see him again. She knew he had sought her out after never hearing from her. But she figured he wouldn't come back here after that considering his broken relationship with his dad.

"Melissa?"

Her name. His voice.

Closing her eyes, it was like they were eighteen all over again. Planning their future together. Her eyes moved from the chair to the floor and froze when they reached his old work boots. Taking a deep breath, she made her way up his dark jeans, past his green cotton button down shirt, and rested on his deep blue eyes. The same blue eyes from her dreams. They took her breath away. His hair was cut shorter than she remembered, but still looked messy on the top.

"Blake." His name was almost a whisper as she spoke.

A smile stretched across his face and he never broke eye contact. It was like they were suspended in time, the only ones in the coffee shop. All the hopes and dreams she had once held on to crashed around in her mind. He looked good, amazing actually. His arms and shoulders had filled out. Gone was the lanky baseball player who stole her heart.

"Do you mind if I join you?" he asked.

"Um, of course not," she said hoping her voice was as steady as the chair she was leaning against. How long had she dreamed of having another chance to sit down and talk with him? She closed her journal and pulled her empty tea cup close. He took a seat across from her and sat his drink down.

"Are you still writing?" Blake asked nodding to her closed journal.

Hesitant, she finally found her voice. "Uh, yeah. I still carry it with me everywhere." She slid the worn leather into her purse and laid her hands on her lap.

"I see that your drink of choice hasn't changed," she said eyeing his cup of coffee.

He smiled, "No, some things never change. I guess it's just too good to surrender and move on to another one. It'd be like I wasn't being true to myself." They both smiled. His words settled heavy on her heart. They sat in silence for a moment, causing her spine to tense against the chair back.

She broke eye contact and released a deep breath. Had it really been eight years since she'd heard his voice or seen his eyes? She eyed the door and bit her tongue debating how many steps it would take her to make it outside. The fear of what he'd think if he knew the reasons behind her leaving him made her want to bolt. But at the same time, how many times had Melissa dreamed of getting to be near Blake one more time? The possibility that he wouldn't judge her made her heart skip with hope. Then she saw the strong jaw and thick shoulders and she's reminded of the lost time that's now between them. Pushing the fear back she looked up at him.

"Well, I'm glad to see that the military hasn't changed everything about you." She said it before she thought about it. "I-I'm sorry. I didn't mean that in a bad way."

His smile was tender, while he seemed to be looking for something to say. She tried not to stare long but it was hard not to notice how good he looked. The military definitely made him grow up and he looked the part.

He rested his arms on the table and said, "It's ok. The Marines pride themselves on building boys into strong men and that requires some change."

She returned his smile. She had definitely changed and it was clear that Blake had too. Deep down she felt like she could still see the same Blake she knew all those years ago, or so she hoped. She cleared her throat. "What brings you back to town?"

"It's my dad. He's sick." He looked down and rubbed his hands together. "He found out about 6 months ago."

She didn't expect that. "I'm sorry, Blake. I thought… Has he been released?"

He took a deep breath. "No. He was at the Tarrant County Jail. He was able to get them to award him a compassionate release. The court can grant an inmate an immediate release if their circumstance has dramatically changed. He's recently been transferred to the Dallas Cancer Center because he needs around the clock care."

He paused. "He has lung cancer." The sadness behind the thin veil that was his smile made her heart ache. He always seemed to be able to hide his pain from others, but not her.

At a loss for words, she could only find one thing to say. "I'm so sorry, Blake."

He simply nodded and took a drink of his coffee.

For as long as she could remember, Blake's father was a rough character. He lived a very selfish life full of smoking and alcohol which drove him to verbal and physical abuse. Their senior year of high school, Blake's mom overdosed on prescription pills. As a result, Blake's dad spiraled out of control leading him further into drugs and then a hefty stint in jail. He may not have been the best father by a long shot but he was the only family Blake had.

"Uh, how long are you here for?" she asked.

"I got here yesterday. I'm not sure what my plans are just yet. There's a lot to consider here and back in North Carolina. I just don't know."

"Aren't you still active?" she asked.

"No. I got out after I found out about dad. My Sergeant is encouraging me to take a civilian position as a veteran's assistance specialist. He put in a good word for me and I'm thinking about it. Plus, I bought a house there a few years back."

So, he's not staying. Melissa tried to mask her disappointment. "That sounds great."

His tone dropped. "The doctors haven't given dad very long. Possibly just a few months. Since he was in jail they didn't discover it in time to do much of anything. He's been doing treatments for about two months. I stopped by late last night, but he was tired and fell asleep shortly after I got there." Blake's eyes were strong, yet shadowed by a brokenness.

Her heart ached for him. If only she was still the girl in his life that could comfort him like she used to. But she wasn't sure that'd be possible again even though she wanted to.

She looked down at the remnants of tea swirled at the bottom of her cup. There was no sense of symmetry or direction in the swirls. That's what her life had felt like eight years ago. She imagined that Blake was hurt and confused by her silence and refusal to talk to him. To make the best of a bad situation, she'd given up her dream of writing in a big city and moved back home. Even though leaving Blake was something she had yet to recover from, at the time she thought it was for the best. He was just starting out in the Marines and she didn't want to be a burden to him.

"I'm glad you were able to come home. I truly am sorry." She hoped he believed her.

His blue eyes couldn't hide the thunderstorm deep behind them. They used to be close enough to ask what it was, but her own guilt held her tongue captive. As she saw a slight glimpse of his soul she wondered if he could see hers. She felt so many emotions sitting across from him. There was relief that he had made a life for himself, a sorrow for his reason being back, a sadness that she had missed so much of his life, a brokenness that her decision was the reason for their tension, and a gut-wrenching guilt that he was in the dark about their break up. It wouldn't be a surprise if he could tell seeing him was having an effect on her. It was a mixture of longing and regret.

"How has life treated you?" she asked.

He leaned back in his chair and rubbed his hands on his legs. "Oh, so so. Basic training was good for me I think. Dad didn't come to my graduation of course, but I learned a lot about myself and who I could be."

She instantly felt guilty that he probably didn't have anyone there for him at graduation. She had planned on going up until a few weeks before when she found out she was pregnant. The shock and fear had crippled her. Blake deserved to be excited about his future. She couldn't bring herself to burden him with the brokenness in her heart and responsibility of raising a stranger's baby.

He continued, "I spent some time overseas and moved around several times. I saw a lot of the world, more than anyone should really."

She could tell there was more to that and she was curious as to what it was. What had happened? What had he seen? How did it affect him? She lost the right to ask those questions a long time ago. Maybe with him being back in Shaw Creek she would get the chance to at least be his friend. "I guess both our lives took turns neither of us saw coming."

"I guess so." Blake's face softened and she could see what appeared to be sadness. "I've missed this."

Her heart pulled at his words. He held her eyes and she could see the emotion in them. "Me too," she whispered. There was so much to say, but she couldn't find the words.

"What about you?" His eyes were soft and there was a longing in them. She was surprised they weren't filled with anger and bitterness.

She shifted in her seat. "I'm good. I'm on summer break from teaching English at the high school here in town. I just finished my third year there. During the summer, I help tutor at the library and write columns for the Press." Looking at her cup she smiled. "I really love it."

"That's great." His voice sounded sincere. She looked up and met his warm eyes. He tilted his head to the left and continued, "You know I always thought that you would be some big-time writer for a magazine or something. Perhaps a journalist for some network. Teaching wasn't something I ever pictured you doing. I figured you'd write your way to some big magazine in New York for sure."

Just tell him. She wasn't sure she was ready to tell him everything. She dreaded telling him about college and the horrible night that altered her entire life. He was the only man she'd ever loved and yet she pushed him away. It was something she would always regret. The pit in her stomach threatened to swallow her whole.

Clearing her throat, she said, "I double majored in English and Education. Mom still teaches and so I went with that. It's a good family job. I get holidays and summers off. And I really fell in love with helping kids." She paused a moment and knew she had to tell him about Wyatt. Panic began to rise in her chest. They were in a public place and she could feel the tears prick the back of her eyes. "Some things happened that changed my life, my entire life. So, I had to change as well."

Blake nodded. "Well," he paused as if struggling to say something. "If you're happy then I'm happy for you." His smile was sad. He was hurt and she could tell. She knew he wanted to know more. He deserved that.

She took a deep breath bracing to tell him. "Blake, I need to tell you that I've got a special little man—"

Ring Ring. His phone sounded in his pocket and he looked torn on answering it. "Melissa, I'm so sorry it's my Sergeant again."

"It's ok. Please, answer it." She slumped in her chair. The courage she had just mustered evaporated, leaving her emotionally wrung.

He hesitated a moment before answering. "Knoll speaking." He looked out the window as he listened. "I'm in the middle of—." Blake straightened his shoulders. "Hold on, sir."

Melissa had a feeling their conversation was over. She felt half relief and disappointment.

Blake covered the speaker at the bottom of his phone. "I'm so sorry about this. This is kind of an important call. I've been putting him off."

Melissa held up her hand. "Don't worry, Blake. I understand."

He held her eyes for a few seconds. He cleared his throat and said, "I'm sorry." He stood but paused before turning. "It was good to see you."

"You too." She returned his sad smile. "Maybe we'll get to see each other again?"

He nodded. "I'd like that. I'll stop by and we can hang out or grab lunch. If that's ok?"

"I'd really like that."

Blake paused and for a moment, she thought he might reach for her. He released a deep breath and said, "Bye, Mel." He turned and walked out the front door talking on his phone.

She watched him as he walked to the street corner, took the crosswalk, and disappeared behind the buildings. She stared at the edge of the building for several minutes. He had approached her and asked to have a conversation with her. She'd figured he'd been hurt and grown to hate her for leaving him with no explanation. Seeing him made her realize just how much she'd missed him. It was something she pushed in the back of her mind to try to escape the guilt and regret. Someone bumped into her table and she once again returned to the coffee shop.

She checked the clock on her phone and figured it was time to head out before they started charging her rent for this table. She also had to get to the library to pick Wyatt up.

Chapter 3

Blake Knoll felt the air get pressed out of his lungs by the heaviness as he entered his father's hospital room. It was cold and stale with only the beeps of machines showing any sign of life. He figured visiting his dad wouldn't get any easier. Last night he was there for not even thirty minutes before his dad fell asleep. He still wasn't sure if visiting him every day was going to be something he could do. He made his way over to the chair next to his dad's side. The man lying in the bed was a far cry from the bully he had known as a kid. Blake never expected much out of his dad. Their past was full of broken promises and failed attempts at any kind of relationship.

Blake was in Germany after his last mission when he heard about his dad being sick. The news was a surprise to him since it had been years since he'd spoken to his dad. There were a lot of things to consider before coming home. He had commitments that spanned over several areas of his life: physically, emotionally, and legally. He had the offer of a civilian job, his ex-girlfriend, Jennifer, and the house he bought in hopes of starting a new life. He knew that when he left Europe his service would be over. It was a decision he weighed for the past six months and he was ready to leave the Marines.

He had pushed the resentment and anger he had towards his dad deep into the shadows of his heart. He believed it was his duty as a son to at least make sure his dad's affairs were in order, even though his dad hadn't even cared to make sure Blake was taken care of as a kid. But as the months went by, Blake's feelings began to change. Surprisingly, he felt guilty the man who left him alone was going to face the end of his life alone.

Blake slowly walked across the cool grey tile floor and looked at the picture at the head of his dad's hospital bed. It was a beautiful two story home with a large front porch and two rocking chairs. The house over looked a large body of water, a lake probably. It was a home anyone would be happy to have. Blake shook his head knowing that dream hadn't existed for him. Not yet. He didn't have the happy house with loving parents as a child. The belief that he'd have that happily ever after evaporated when Melissa shut him out of her life.

Then he met Jennifer.

She was pretty and very outgoing. She was the first woman since Melissa who he thought he could see a future with. He decided to buy a house about twenty minutes from base for the possibility of building a life with her one day. But that wasn't meant to be either. He was given a weekend of leave and he decided to return home to surprise her. He'll never forget walking in and finding her legs wrapped around another man in his bed. Maybe happily ever after wasn't in the cards for him. He never dated anyone else long term after that.

Looking down at the bed, Blake focused on his dad's chest rising and falling. All he could do was watch the man he barely knew take weak breaths. He didn't want to wake him because rest was imperative at this point. The only light being let in was from between the blinds on the window and the blinking lights of the machines. Because his father abused everyone that wanted to be close to him there was no one left other than his only son. A son who he made feel he was a mistake, an embarrassment, and never good enough.

Most every night his father would come home angry at the world. It didn't matter how well his mother had tried to pick up the house or how good the grades were on Blake's report card. Blake practiced so hard and became the varsity pitcher as a sophomore. He worked hard to develop his skill. But his dad only saw the errors and never gave a compliment.

The weight of the past closed in on Blake like a noose around his neck. He couldn't swallow for fear he would choke. There were no good memories that came to mind. None. His childhood had been harsh. Something he wouldn't wish on anyone. He could hear the screams, feel the slaps, and see the empty seat next to his mother at the baseball games. His past was a revolving door of anger, bitterness, doubt, and disappointment. The only light and saving grace had been the Adairs. Melissa Adair.

After running into her that morning, he couldn't get her out of his mind. He knew that coming home would bring up his past but he never thought that would involve Melissa. He thought about the time they shared together, and the even longer time they spent apart. He thought about the ache in his heart when she wouldn't speak to him. The panic rose in his chest at the thought that she'd decided not to wait for him to come back like he'd promised. Did she not believe him? Had she met someone else at college? He was positive he hadn't seen a ring on her finger. The thought of her with anyone else was devastating.

Her life was nothing like what she'd said she wanted, even without him. He wondered why she was still in Shaw Creek and teaching of all things. She seemed genuinely happy about it but at the same time he thought he picked up on the loss of a dream, the one she always talked about. The dream she was headed off for when he last saw her. Why had that really not worked out? She said things happened, but what things?

He sighed and looked past his dad's bed to see a dark frame hanging on the far wall of the hospital room. It would've been easy to miss because it was covered by the door when opened. He adjusted his eyes to focus on the image inside and noticed it was a painting. It was a young girl walking down a path through sunflowers, a Monte piece. The picture brought him immediately back to a young girl he once knew who loved being with sunflowers. A girl who let the sunflowers be a sanctuary for him as well.

On nights when his dad came home drunk, he would yell and beat Blake's mom first. When Blake stepped in to stop him, all the anger would turn toward him. The only escape was the friendship he found with Melissa. Once his dad collapsed on the sofa in a drunken sleep and he saw his mom was tucked in bed, Blake would run down the street past Melissa's grandparents' house into their sunflower field. He used to run as fast as he could, praying all the pain and anger would be ripped away in the passing wind as he made his way to their special spot. There he would grab the flashlight hidden in the oak's nook to send a signal to her bedroom window across the field. She would signal him back and soon she would come running through the sunflowers to meet him. It was in those moments where he felt the most peace, acceptance, and love.

"Blake?" His dad stirred in the bed and their eyes met. "Are you ok, son?"

Leaning forward, Blake cleared his throat. "I'm just thinking. How are you feeling today?"

His father grinned. "I'm good. Well, as good as you could expect. What's on your mind?"

This was something new. His dad never asked how he was doing. Just hearing it made Blake feel awkward. Sharing was something that he always wanted, but never got the chance to do. It didn't come to him naturally and it surprised him that his dad even asked.

"Oh, nothing."

His dad strained to take a deep breath. "I would like to know. Please?"

Blake swallowed hard. What could it hurt to open up a little with his dad? In the past he would've criticized or discouraged Blake no matter what he said, if he even really listened at all. Deep down, Blake wanted to share with his dad. He wasn't sure being open with his dad would pay off but in that moment, he thought why not. He took a deep breath and took the chance. "Do you remember, Melissa Adair?"

"Oh yes. Your friend from high school. Pretty girl." His father nodded. "What about her?"

"Well, I happened to run into her this morning."

"Really? What has it been four... five years?"

"Eight. It's been eight years. I haven't seen her since the night before I left for basic." Blake couldn't expect his dad to remember much. Back then he saw everything through the bottom of his whisky bottle.

"Why do you seem troubled about it?" His dad seemed to care. Maybe now he really did.

Blake rested his elbows on his knees. "I guess I just didn't expect to see her. She always wanted to go write for a big publishing company in Chicago or New York."

"Perhaps she's visiting."

Hesitant, Blake answered, "She said she was teaching at our old high school. Last I knew she was going to school for journalism not education. I guess something happened and she changed her mind."

His dad nodded and looked up at the ceiling. Once again Blake studied the man. For the first time in Blake's life his dad needed him. Their relationship had the opportunity to become something. It appeared that his dad was making the effort and so maybe Blake should do the same. It wasn't perfect and this was only the second time he had seen his dad in years. Whether he admitted it or not, he was glad he was here.

A tall man in a white coat entered the room. "Mr. Knoll, how are we doing today?" He paused when he saw Blake sitting next to his dad. "You must be Blake." Blake stood and took the man's hand. "I'm Dr. Bill Jackson. I'm overseeing your father's treatment."

"It's nice to meet you, sir. Blake Knoll."

"Your dad has talked a lot about you. You're in the U.S. Marine Corp, is that correct?"

Blake nodded. "Yes, sir. Raiders Special Forces."

"Your dad told me that you'd been offered a job working with the Veteran Affairs office." Dr. Jackson slid his hands in his coat pockets.

"Well, my Sergeant put in a good word for me but there's no definite offer just yet."

"I wanted to see if you'd be interested in volunteering at the V.A. hospital. The physical therapy ward is needing some extra hands and someone like you would be perfect. It's a little more hands on and one on one."

His dad spoke up for the first time since the doctor came into the room. "I think you'd be really good at it. It's a volunteer spot so there's no long-term commitment. It would give you something to do while back in Texas."

The idea really intrigued Blake. The job opportunity as a veteran's assistance specialist in North Carolina was helping with coordinate and instruct counseling groups for service members to transition back into civilian life. The negative is it didn't seem as personal. Helping with hands on physical therapy would allow him to help veterans individually and walk with them through their treatment and recovery.

"That sounds like a great program. Sure, I'd like to go visit the ward and meet with them," Blake said.

His dad beamed with pride. "Great."

Dr. Jackson smiled and said, "Wonderful. I'll let them know you're interested in volunteering. Just give them your name at check in and they will be able to get you upstairs." Once he was finished checking all the machines the doctor excused himself from the room.

The next few hours went by quicker than Blake expected. There was one thing that brought them to a common ground and it was the Texas Wranglers baseball. They were able to bond even if only in the silence listening to the announcer on the TV. Blake could see his dad struggling to stay awake to watch the game. He lasted longer than Blake had expected.

Looking at his watch, Blake turned to his dad, "Well, Dad, I believe they'll be bringing you dinner shortly. I haven't eaten much at all myself. I'll see you tomorrow."

His dad reached over and patted Blake's hands. "Thank you, son."

On his way toward the elevators he decided to grab a water out of the vending machine. As he bent down to retrieve the bottle he heard a familiar voice.

"Blake? Blake Knoll?"

He turned with water in hand, "Cami?" He gave her a quick hug. "I would ask what you're doing here but based on the scrubs, I think I know. Wow, I didn't know you were a nurse."

As Melissa's older sister, Blake knew a lot about Cami but didn't see her much. She was off at college by the time he and Melissa became close. She had Melissa's big brown eyes, but her hair was lighter and shorter.

She smiled, "Yeah, I really love it. It's the biggest blessing to be able to serve people and maybe help save a life." The passion was evident in her eyes. She paused. "Uh, what about you? What are you doing here? I feel like I haven't seen you in forever."

"Yeah it's been a while. My dad has been transferred here for treatment." He shoved one hand in his pocket and gripped the bottle in the other.

Her eyes softened, "I'm so sorry, Blake. I had no idea." Her empathy was evident as her shoulders dropped. "Are you on leave?"

"Uh, no. I didn't extend my service and got out a few months ago. I've moved back into my dad's house. Dr. Jackson also got me the opportunity to help at the V.A. hospital while I'm here."

"That's great. I'm sure you'll be great with their patients," she said sincerely.

Blake dropped his eyes to his bottle. "I ran into Melissa this morning."

Cami shifted her weight. "Oh you did?"

"Yeah, it was nice to see her." Trying to avoid the awkward silence he continued, "I didn't know that she was living here and teaching English at the high school. I didn't expect to run into her."

Cami smiled and nodded. "Yeah she really loves it."

Blake felt like she was purposefully not saying much. That made him question things even more. "I'm just surprised... you know."

Cami took a deep breath. "I understand the questions you probably have Blake, really I do. I would agree with you that you have a right to want to know them. But it's not my story to tell."

Blake dropped his shoulders. He figured she wouldn't tell him much and of course she would talk to Melissa about seeing him.

"It was really good to see you, Blake. I guess I will probably be seeing you around here. Again, I'm so sorry about your dad." With that she was gone, disappearing down the hall into the bustle of other nurses and doctors.

As Blake made his way out of the hospital, he found himself questioning things more than ever. The conversation with his sergeant, the possible job, his relationship with his dad, and then Melissa. In fact, his relationship with his dad was clearer than the answers he desperately wanted from Melissa.

Chapter 4

Fumbling with his keys, Blake stepped out of his truck and onto his dad's driveway. He closed the door and looked across the street. Mrs. Meyers was watering her flower bed and tugging at one of the chains holding a basket. He ran across his yard and crossed their dead-end road.

"Let me get that for you, Mrs. Meyers." He grabbed the bottom of the basket and readjusted the chain.

"Why thank you, Blake. But there's no need for this 'Mrs.' business. You can still call me Gram." She set her water pot down on the porch, then turned and gave him a warm hug only a grandmother could give. "I thought I saw someone over at your dad's yesterday. I didn't know it was you. The military looks good on you I must say. How are you, dear?"

As his childhood neighbor and Melissa's grandmother, Mrs. Meyers had been very good to him. She was always so caring and interested in what Blake was doing. He smiled to himself, some things never change. He dropped one foot off the porch and rested against one of the pillars. "Thank you. I don't regret my time serving. It was definitely something I needed to do." He swallowed hating the repeated explanation of his return to Shaw Creek. "I got out of the Marines a few months ago and am temporarily staying at Dad's. That way I can be here for him. He has cancer."

She placed her hand gently on his arm. Gram looked tenderly in his eyes as though they were a doorway to his soul. "I'm so sorry, child." Gram dropped her hand and turned looking toward his home. "I know that you may not feel this way but your father probably does appreciate you being here." She met his eyes again. "Your heart is beautiful for being here for him. Will you please let me know if there is anything I can do for you?" She reached for his hand and clasped it tightly. "Know that you don't have to be alone in this."

Blake wasn't so sure he agreed with her. His heart shuddered at the thought of really letting anyone walk this path with him. When he was a kid the Adairs and Meyers were so good to him. After returning home to find Melissa and them turning him away, he was hesitant to let them in close enough to help with his dad. Melissa's rejection along with her family's left deep scars. Helping someone else wasn't even a question but opening himself to the same was a different story.

He gave her a wry smile. "I appreciate it."

"What are you doing while you're here?"

"Well, I'm going to be volunteering at the V.A. hospital helping with therapy and spending time with Dad."

She smiled brightly at him. "That's wonderful, Blake. Are you looking for a job?"

He shrugged and said, "Not sure yet. I still have some things back in North Carolina that need to be taken care of. There is a civilian job on base that I've applied for, but it's all up in the air. So, I haven't decided what I'm going to do long term."

"Well, I hope you know you are more than welcome in my home." He was a little surprised at her statement, but knew she was an honest woman. Her face dropped slightly. "I know it may not have seemed like it the last time you were here but our family loves you, Blake. *All* our family."

He felt a lump grow in his throat. He batted his emotions back down and cleared his throat. His eyes turned toward the north side of her house. "There is something that I would like to ask you." He met her eyes again.

"Sure, dear. What is it?"

"Would you mind if I took walks through the sunflower field?"

Her eyes were bright and smile warm. "Of course not. Anytime." She didn't have to say anything else.

Blake knew Gram and he had an understanding where comfort, grace, and peace met. And for both of them it was in the sunflowers.

"Thank you." He stepped off the porch and hesitated to keep walking. He looked back at Mrs. Meyers and she nodded. Blake had missed her tender heat and wisdom. She always gave so much to everyone. He smiled, then turned and headed north.

Blake stopped at the edge of the sunflowers. The flowers always towered over his head as a kid and now was no different. His memory of this place was something he never wanted to change. What would he find? What would he feel once he crossed the yellow threshold? No matter what it was, he felt the pull of something greater than himself and he couldn't stop now.

With each step Blake walked through the sunflowers and felt at home. It was something he had missed. Something he longed for. They were bright, strong, and tall, all things he wanted to be when he was young. Perhaps then he would've been able to stand up to his dad and really protect his mom. He made his way down the long rows until they opened up in a small clearing with a pond. He stopped in his tracks. Floods of memories wrapped around him like his old letterman jacket, comfortable and full. He stood there for a long time just staring. It was the safest place on earth. He couldn't hear his dad's screams, his mother's cries, or the fears behind his own eyes. It was surprising how nothing had changed.

Blake made his way to the oak tree separating the sunflowers from the pond. He smiled when he saw the old tire swing was still there. He walked over, noticing that the spot where he and Melissa used to sit was still worn down. It was almost like they had been there last night instead of eight years ago. His eyes traveled up to the notch a little over half way up to the first branch and he reached in. The tips of his fingers ran over something he had hoped to find, but was certain wasn't there. Slowly he pulled the two items from the notch. Stepping back away from the tree he stared at the objects in his hand.

He sat down at the base letting the tree cradle his back like he remembered. Placing the flashlight on the ground, Blake held the pocket watch in the tips of his fingers. He pressed the release and it opened. All three hands remained still above the face. On the adjacent side was the same old picture of Pops and Gram. Their young faces were full of life and love. Holding his breath, he slid his fingernail under the bottom of the picture and lifted. His inhale caught. Underneath was *their* picture. He was almost sure it would've been discarded. Two kids young and in love. They were sitting at the oak tree, her head on his shoulder, her eyes bright, her smile worth a million bucks, and her hair flowing over her shoulders.

"Melissa."

Blake's heart ached for more than one reason. Being back here and actually seeing Melissa had brought back old feelings. Feelings he thought he had let go, but deep down knew he never really would. When he first met Melissa, he never thought she'd stick with him after finding out about his family. She had the perfect life with parents, though they were divorced, who loved her and supported everything she did. They were religious and respectable, the exact opposite of his. Regardless, somewhere along the way she fell for him.

Why didn't she wait for him and trust him to come back to her?

Blake ran this thumb across their picture. Melissa was kind, loving, and beautiful. The best thing was she seemed to be clueless of this. She used to blush when someone would compliment her and wave them off. He loved that about her. If he was honest with himself, he loved everything about her. Even more than that, Blake loved who he was when he was with her. She had supported him and encouraged him to be better than his circumstances. She said she was ok with him enlisting and was great all the way up until he was half way through basic. He told her once he got settled that he would come back for her and they could get married. He knew that she could write from anywhere and he believed that she would be happy. She said she agreed.

At first, he couldn't understand why she never responded to his letters while he was in basic. It was hard to write with their strict schedule, but he did send her seven letters with no response. He even sent her the information so she could come to the graduation. He knew his dad wouldn't be there and he honestly didn't want anyone other than Melissa.

Looking back, it was understandable to see that their lives were being pulled in different directions. He knew she probably made new friends and a new life in college. She was a beautiful girl and the fact that she didn't think so made her even more attractive. If there was ever anyone who needed a friend she was one to help them. She was very likable. It was possible she met someone that first semester and she didn't want to wait for him. But he was positive he didn't see a ring on her finger, he made sure to look. Maybe she realized she couldn't do the long-distance thing. They had discussed him enlisting at length before he did it. And they discussed all the different scenarios that might occur. She was supportive the whole time. She said she loved him and he believed her because he loved her too.

The pit in his stomach crept up into his throat again. No matter how hard he tried to tell himself he didn't, he still cared deeply for Melissa. He hated to think about her loving someone else. It had taken him a long time to even think about her loving someone else. He definitely couldn't.

He ran his thumb over the picture again. Their conversation that morning had been nice and surprisingly easy. He had lived a lot of life and he figured she had as well. The fact was both of them had changed. They really didn't know that much about each other... anymore.

A hawk's cry overhead brought Blake back from his thoughts. The sun was setting and he remembered he hadn't eaten anything since lunch. He closed the watch and hopped to his feet. Returning the items to the notch, Blake turned and made his way back through the sunflowers. This beautiful place he had long ago left was the only thing he could see hadn't changed. Nothing in Shaw Creek was the same except for the peace in this spot.

As he broke through the sunflowers and found the street, he knew that Melissa may not be willing to share her feelings or spend time with him but regardless, he sure hoped he'd run into her again.

Chapter 5

A cool north breeze swept through the sunflowers and into Gram's backyard. Melissa and Cami sat on the swing gently gliding as they watched James and Wyatt playing catch. Wyatt had a baseball game in a few days and James was the team coach. Any time he and Cami stopped by they *had* to get some extra practice in. Wyatt sure loved having his soon-to-be uncle James around. Melissa's mom, Julie, and Gram came outside to join them with a pitcher of sweet tea and some iced glasses. Her mom poured one for everyone.

Julie Meyers-Adair, was a beautiful, strong woman. After Melissa's dad walked out on them eight years ago, the year before Melissa had Wyatt, Julie made the decision to move back in with Gram. Once she found out she was pregnant with Wyatt, Melissa didn't know what to do, she chose to move back home and finish college at a smaller school. Melissa liked to think that she got her strength from her mom. Being a single mother, she needed support and both Gram and Julie had given it to her. They never once judged her or told her how horrible it was that she was moving back home. It was never a problem for her to change her major and career path for something more parent friendly. There was always support and love from both her mom and Gram. A debt Melissa could never repay.

"How are my two favorite girls doing today?" Julie asked handing them each a glass.

"Good." Both Cami and Melissa said in unison.

"How did your meeting with the florist go, Cami?" Julie took her seat next to Gram.

After taking a big drink Cami answered, "Great! I got everything ordered and the flowers should be here the week of the wedding so we can go by and see them."

"That's great," Julie took her own drink. "And how is the summer youth program, Mel?"

"The kids are doing really well. The math and science teacher said Wyatt is doing good, which makes me happy since I'm no help in those areas." She looked out at her son, who was laughing at something James had just said.

Gram followed her eyes to the boys in the yard. "He sure loves baseball."

Melissa nodded. "That he does."

A comfortable silence settled on the women as they sipped their tea and rocked gently in the much appreciated summer breeze. Gram and Julie began talking about the church service that morning. After a few minutes Cami shifted on the swing but kept her eyes on the boys. She lowered her voice and said, "I heard you ran into Blake after I left the coffee shop the other day."

Melissa sighed. "Yes."

"How did that go?"

"It was better than I bet you're imagining. He was very nice and it didn't appear that he was angry, which is what I had always expected." Melissa knew that if he was angry it would be understandable. But he hadn't pressed her much at all.

"I can understand that." Cami paused for a moment. "He wanted to ask me what happened. I could tell."

Melissa turned her head to look at Cami who likewise turned to look at her. They stared at each other for a moment before Cami continued. "He wants to know why you never responded to him. He was surprised you're teaching too."

Melissa dropped her head and stared at the glass of tea in her lap. She could feel the tears building and she willed them back. She knew that he would have questions. She remembered the longing she saw in his eyes at the coffee shop. Telling him the answers terrified her.

"What are you going to do?" Cami turned to look back out at James and Wyatt.

"I've spent thousands of hours thinking about what I'd say if I ever got the chance. It's terrifying to think about what he will think. I don't know if I can handle him hating me because I didn't give him the option to stay in my life." Two tears made their escape down her cheeks. "I almost told him in the coffee shop. I wasn't prepared and was panicking. Then he got an important call and had to leave."

Cami tucked her arm under Melissa's and squeezed their elbows together. "I understand that fear. It's easier to look at him and know that you made the decision to not have the relationship. I don't judge you for that choice because I don't know what I would do in the same situation. Rape is a horrible thing and it wasn't your fault some scumbag dropped that crap in your drink. But you and Blake are older now, no longer kids fresh out of high school. What if he isn't angry? What if he respects your choice once he knows why you did it?"

Melissa's heart lifted at the thought. Is that not what she had always wanted? She wanted to have Blake in her life and to tell him what happened, why she was silent, and how she still felt about him. But would he see her as still worth it? "I don't even know that he still has feelings for me. Maybe he just asked you that for closure to be able to move on."

"Well, is he seeing anyone?" Cami asked.

"That wasn't one of the topics we discussed." Though Melissa had thought about it several times since seeing him.

"Did he have a ring on?"

Melissa shook her head. "No."

"So you looked?" Cami smiled

"Of course I looked." Melissa ran her finger along the top rim of her tea glass. The idea of Blake falling in love with someone else was something she basically already accepted. She figured after all these years he'd be married with children living far off on some military base. It tore her heart apart just thinking about it, but what could she expect. She was the reason they weren't together.

"Well, there you go," Cami smirked.

Melissa sighed. "That doesn't mean he doesn't have someone waiting for him. I don't even know where he's been or where he'll end up."

"He told me he didn't re-enlist after hearing about his dad. He was nice in his conversation with you and I could tell there was something in the way he asked me about you. Once you talk to him things will be clearer for you both."

Melissa closed her eyes as another breeze swept past them. The emotion they both seemed to be struggling with had to mean something, didn't it? Plus, she hadn't revealed the biggest part of her life now, Wyatt. "What if Wyatt is a deal breaker for him?"

"I get that some guys don't want to take on another man's child. But you don't know that Blake is like that. What if he surprises you? What if he is happy about Wyatt?"

Cami rested her head against Melissa's shoulder and then she asked the one question that was buried deep in Melissa's heart. "What if he still loves you too?"

Chapter 6

Melissa stood in front of the small room full of grade school students. "Ok, let's move on to the next worksheet. This time we will be reading the section at the top and then writing about what you read. I'll let you know when your time is up." Once she got the boys to stop laughing in the back they got right to work.

Melissa returned her papers to the front table. She took a drink of water from her bottle and looked out over the kids. The room was a lot smaller than her classroom. There weren't any big windows either, which made it seem dark. The library had long tables instead of individual desks and there was no board to write examples for the kids to see. The space was small as it was a spare room in the back of the library. But none of that mattered to Melissa. She was happy that their small town was able to help kids engage in different subjects over the summer if desired. Though they were younger than her usual students, she still felt comfortable in front of them.

There was a light knock on the door and Melissa looked up to see Jade McBride, her best friend. She checked to make sure all the kids were busy working and then stepped just outside the open door.

"Hey, girl." Jade gave her a hug. "I was wondering when you were working up here."

"Yeah this week starts their language arts and reading tutoring. I'm up here three days a week."

"I saw Wyatt over at the computers." Jade motioned behind them.

"Yeah, he is in a different group of students than my class. What did you bring for lunch?"

"Chicken pitas and fruit medley." Jade handed Melissa a small brown bag with a circle logo for Jade's Gem on the front. Jade was another big help in making this summer youth program work because she donated the lunches from her diner.

"Oh, yum!" Melissa opened the bag and looked inside. "You've done a great job helping out donating lunches for this program." Jade gave her a big cheesy grin that made Melissa chuckle. "Hey, how did Andrew's business pitch go in San Antonio?"

Jade rolled her eyes. "Good, I guess. He got back Saturday morning and had to leave again Monday for Atlanta. He's always busy coming and going on different business trips it's been tough the past few weeks. Sometimes I wonder if we're on the same page for what we want our future to be."

Andrew Perry wasn't Melissa's favorite pick for Jade. She wanted Jade to be with someone who was home more and made time for her. Jade deserved someone who would adore her and shower her with love. That's what Melissa wanted. Andrew just seemed to worry more about himself.

"You've been dating for two years now. This season of life is just harder. It's like you're waiting for the first day of spring to put an end to winter."

"I'm sure you're right." Jade nodded.

"You know I love you, right? I just want you to be sickeningly happy." Melissa winked at Jade.

"Well, we have been honorary sisters since eighth grade, the first person we share the tears and laughs with, college roommates, and I wouldn't expect anything less from you."

Melissa could only pray she was as good a friend to Jade as Jade had been to her. Jade was there for her when Blake left for basic. Jade was the one to rescue her from a stranger's bedroom the night she was raped. She was there to hug Melissa as she gave birth to Wyatt. Jade was her very best friend.

"Ms. Adair, I brought doughnuts and left them in the librarian's office." Melissa looked over Jade's shoulder to see Mark Johnson.

"Thanks, Mr. Johnson."

He smiled at her and then moved down the hall to where his class was meeting in another conference room.

"Who was that?" Jade asked.

"Mark Johnson, he works at the middle school, but he's helping with the science and math kids this summer."

"He likes you."

Melissa huffed, "Whatever. I'm not interested, so it doesn't matter."

"You may have to tell him that one day." Jade's face changed suddenly to something more mischievous. "So word on the street is that there's a super-hot Marine staying in town. In fact, I believe he's staying across the street from you. You wouldn't happen to know anything about that, would you?" Jade crossed her arms and smirked.

Melissa checked on the kids again, then took another step away from the door to give them some more privacy. "You heard?"

"Of course I heard. You know where I work. Gossip Central. Have you seen him?"

Melissa sighed, "Yes. I ran into him at the coffee shop a few days ago."

"And he talked to you?"

"Yes. He approached me and we had a nice talk. His dad has cancer. He's back to be there for his dad and to tend to his estate." She fidgeted with the hem of her blouse. "I didn't tell him about Wyatt. By the way our conversation went I don't think he has a clue."

"Why didn't you?"

"That's everyone's question." Melissa wrapped her arms around her torso.

It wasn't that Melissa was ashamed of Wyatt. She just didn't know how to have that conversation with Blake. Not that she hadn't thought a thousand times about what she would say to him to explain the rape and the decisions she made afterward. But in that moment seeing him for the first time in eight years, she wasn't ready and just couldn't do it. She was relieved he got that phone call.

"I couldn't have that talk with him... in public. I know he probably wants to know why I shut him out but I just couldn't." She looked down at the ground.

"He deserves to know don't you think? It's not like he won't find out eventually with you guys living across the street."

"I know." Jade was right. Melissa knew that it would have to happen, she just needed a little more time to think about what to say. Melissa couldn't hide things from Jade. She knew Melissa too well. Jade probably already knew how much Blake being back in town effected Melissa. But the beautiful thing about Jade was she knew just the right amount to push. She was honest and dependable but knew how to back off and give Melissa her space as well.

"Is he single?"

Melissa sighed. "Cami asked me the same question."

Jade raised one eye brow. "Well?"

"He didn't have a ring on if that's what you really want to know. But I don't know anything about his love life." Once again her heart ached at the thought. Melissa peeked in around the corner at the kids and said, "Five more minutes and we will discuss what you wrote." Then she turned back to Jade.

"How did he look?" Jade asked.

Melissa dropped her eyes to the ground.

"That good huh?"

"Yeah." Melissa could see Blake's ocean blue eyes staring at her from across the coffee shop table. His broad shoulders and chest pulling at his shirt. There was no way that some other woman hadn't at least tried to snatch him up.

"I guess the rumors I've heard from other women in the diner are true. They've all said Blake Knoll is hot." Jade paused as if studying Melissa for a moment. "Can I ask you something?"

Melissa, still looking at her feet, nodded and gave their promised answer to that question. "Always."

"Do you still love him?"

Melissa closed her eyes tightly willing the tears to remain at bay. Slowly she raised her head to look at Jade. "More than ever."

Chapter 7

Ding. The shuffle of feet surrounded Blake as he took his last bite of pancake. Jade's Gem was fairly new, or at least new to Blake. The food was great and he felt like he was eating at Mrs. Meyers's kitchen table. He smiled at the memory. His mind was somewhere else. There were so many changes and things he didn't expect when he came home almost a week ago.

Blake had agreed to volunteering at the V.A. hospital three times a week. It had been really rewarding getting to know the patients on a first name basis. It made him think a lot about what he'd want to do with the rest of his life. Now that the active duty was off the table he had to set his sights on something more long term. There was still a major debate about the job opportunity, but Blake was certain that working with veterans was something he'd enjoy.

He had been to see his dad every day, spending several hours with him. Watching the cancer eat at his body wasn't something Blake had really thought about. The hardened heart that had crippled him as a teen and driven him away was starting to dissolve. Along with supporting his dad, there was another skeleton from his past forcing its way to the front line. Melissa.

He took a drink of his water and leaned back against the booth. It had been half a week since he spoke to her. Though he had noticed her staying at her grandmother's house every night. Her mom appeared to be there too along with a young boy not quite ten, Blake figured. It made sense that Julie Adair would move back in to care for her mother in the apparent passing of her father, John Meyers. He figured Melissa was saving money and living with them too. There could be any number of reasons. But who was the boy? Oh, well. He at least got to see Melissa in passing most days. She had waved when she saw him which made him happy.

A young couple sat on the same side of the booth across from Blake. They were giggling and sitting close. He turned to look at his empty booth and sighed. He pulled out his wallet and dug out the only two pictures he kept close. The first was a picture of him and Melissa sitting on her parent's front porch on the 4th of July. Melissa had on a red, white, and blue tie dyed tank top. Her face was bright and made him smile. He looked at himself and his face was equally as happy. The second picture was at the anniversary party for Pop and Gram. Melissa had hopped on his back as they were walking through the sunflower field. They were both laughing. Being with Melissa had been the happiest time in his life.

Blake's emotions in regard to Melissa were a jumbled mess. He hadn't expected to ever see her again. After not hearing from her during and after basic training, he'd hoped and prayed they would be able to make it work. He had tried every angle to get in contact with her, but to no avail. None of his letters were returned so surely she got them, someone did. He even came looking for her once, but that wasn't a success thanks to his dad's ability to ruin every good thing in Blake's life. Once back at his base things picked up and he was sent on several secret missions. Before he knew it, a week had passed, then a month, and then eight years.

Being in Shaw Creek and living across the street from her again, his heart and mind were battling each other. His heart wanted to take her in his arms and love her even more than he had when they were young. His mind told him to be careful because she had the power to crush him all over again. He desperately wanted to talk to her, not just to get answers but to really talk to her. She had been his best friend and he wanted a glimpse of that again. Blake shook his head trying to clear it. He was here to take care of his dad, which was enough of an emotional battle, let alone to even think about Melissa.

Blake maneuvered his way through the line of people waiting and made his way outside. Digging in his pocket for his truck keys another familiar voice caught his attention.

"Blake!"

He turned around. "James Mitchell! It's been forever, man." Blake shook James's right hand and squeezed his shoulder with the left. "How are things?"

"Good. *Really* good." James couldn't contain his happiness. "Better than I can even begin to tell you."

Blake knew what that kind of happiness felt like. "Congrats on the wedding by the way. I saw the announcement in the paper."

"Thanks, man. I bet you were surprised to hear about it?" James's tone was light and familiar.

Blake smiled, realizing how long it'd been since they had hung out. "I was a little. You and Cami Adair? I never would've guessed it. But I am happy for you guys."

Never in his wildest dreams did Blake think that James would settle down before he was forty. He was always running around crazy and doing the party scene. Marriage didn't seem to be on his radar and he'd always teased Blake for wanting to plan a future with Melissa.

"I know, I know," James said in a sarcastic tone. "I guess when it's the right person and the timing is right you just know."

"I guess so," Blake said, nodding and thinking again about Melissa.

"Hey, I'd like to ask you to be an usher at our wedding."

Blake felt good knowing James would ask him. They were old friends and baseball teammates, but had lost touch while he was overseas. "Sure. I'd be honored."

James smiled. "Great! Let me get your number." Blake told it to him and James saved it in his phone. "I'll send you the information for the rehearsal dinner and wedding, or Cami will." Suddenly his face dropped. "She told me about your dad. I'm sorry to hear about everything."

Blake cleared his throat. "Thanks. It's been harder than I'd expected it to be but I'm glad I decided to come."

"You're a good son."

Blake wasn't so sure he believed James. He wanted to be a good son, but his dad had always told him he wasn't. He hadn't been around since leaving for basic and hadn't tried to contact his dad since. Though he was trying to honor the fact that he was the only person his dad had.

James punched Blake in the shoulder like they used to do in high school. "Man, you look good. The military has you all buff. You might finally be able to out hit me now."

"Ha!" Blake huffed. "My baseball swing has always been better than yours."

James shook his head. "I'll let you think that. Hey, have you played much since school?"

"Nah. I have to say I miss it though. The glove, the bat, the smell of the grass, I miss it all. I still try to keep up with the Wranglers though. You?"

"I've been coaching a little league team. And I try to find time to get some swinging practice in." James's voice was upbeat and Blake could tell he was enjoying it.

"You're becoming a real family man, aren't you?"

"I guess so. A little." James looked at his phone. "I got to grab a bite really quick and then meet Cami at the house so we can head to the fields. She worked another twelve-hour shift, but still manages to come out to the games with me. We have a game at Cedar Park ball fields at 2:00pm tomorrow. You should come by and then we can hang out after, like old times."

"Sure. I've started volunteering at the V.A. hospital three times a week and then spend time with dad. I would love to help out at the fields."

"Great," James said and slapped Blake's shoulder as he headed for the diner's door. "I'll see you then. I'm going to grab some of Jade's homemade biscuits and gravy."

"Jade?" Blake asked.

James paused. "Yeah you remember –"

"Well I thought I saw you in my dining room. Blake Knoll."

Blake turned and saw Jade McBride, walking up behind them. Her hair was pulled back into a high bun and she had flour on the front of her shirt and apron.

"I was just about to tell Blake that this was your diner," James said giving Jade a hug.

"Yep. She's all mine." She turned to Blake. "I'm glad you stopped in. I heard you were back in town. I'm sorry about your dad."

Blake figured Melissa had talked to Jade about seeing him. "Thank you."

"Hey, I've got to get some grub and head out. I'm glad I caught you, man. See you later." James shook his hand and disappeared behind the glass doors.

"How are you?" Blake asked Jade.

"I'm good. I work six days a week but business is good. The best part of my job is dealing with the rotten single men hitting on me or my waitresses."

Blake laughed. A lot of things had changed, but it was good to see Jade wasn't one of them. She was a spit fire and a great friend to Melissa. Now she was her very own business owner. "Congratulations on the diner. That's really great."

"Thank you." She paused and Blake could sense the mood change to a little tense. He wanted to ask her about Melissa, but he figured she would do the same as Cami. "Melissa told me she saw you."

"Yeah," Blake said softly.

"I know you must have questions. Melissa, she's been through a lot. There are reasons for the way she handled things after you left.

She may not say it but I know she'll tell you about it. Just give her some time." Jade paused as if studying him for a moment. "Can I ask you something?"

Blake swallowed the lump in his throat and simply nodded.

"Do you still care about her?"

"Yes." Blake didn't even hesitate. The next statement he said with confidence. "I've never stopped."

The corners of Jade's mouth curved up. "I thought so."

Blake could feel a tightness in his chest. Jade always called it like it was and she was very protective of Melissa. It wouldn't be a surprise if Melissa was to find out about this conversation. In fact, he hoped Jade would tell her. Maybe if she knew he still cared about her Melissa would reach out to him.

"It was good to see you, Blake. Give her a little more time." Jade turned and retreated back into her diner.

As he made his way home, Blake's mind was swirling. First, he was happy for James and Cami. It was good to see a couple in love just starting out. He'd be lying to himself if he said he wasn't a little jealous. But something that James had said came to mind.

When it's the right person and the timing is right you just know.

He thought he knew the answer to both those things a long time ago. But he'd been wrong.

Second, Blake thought about Jade and Melissa. Knowing that something had happened to Melissa didn't give him much relief. He hoped she would come to him soon because he wasn't sure how much longer he could keep himself from seeing her again.

He made his way to the front door of his home. His hand frozen on the handle. He didn't know if it would get easier walking through this door, seeing his dad's health fail him, watching friends marry and move on, or even seeing Melissa. But there was one thing he knew for sure, being back home was proof that things and people had moved forward. Perhaps the changes surrounding him weren't as altering as the changes he was beginning to see in himself.

Chapter 8

Wyatt jumped up into his chair at the table and said, "Mornin', Mom!" He was always the happiest kid in the morning. A trait Melissa could only hope would last into his teens.

"I'm getting it." She poured his milk into a glass and placed his plate of eggs, ham, and fruit down in front of him. She fixed her plate the same and joined him at the table. "You sure are happy this morning. Did you sleep good?"

Wyatt started shoveling food into his mouth as if he hadn't eaten in a week. Melissa cleared her throat. Wyatt paused and looked at her. "You forgot to say grace."

He dropped his fork and took her outstretched hand. Melissa tried to hide her amusement when she noticed his heavy sigh. She may not be the best mom in a lot of areas, but she tried really hard to make sure that her son knew the importance of talking to God on a regular basis. Especially when he thought he didn't have time for it. Once they said 'Amen', Wyatt jumped right back into eating.

"So, I take it you slept good."

"Sure," Wyatt answered between bites.

Melissa smiled and shook her head. "Are you ready for your game this morning?"

Wyatt gave her a big grin, "Yep! I've been working on my swing."

"I'm so proud of you. You're getting better all the time," Melissa patted his back and continued to eat her breakfast. His attitude was still pretty good, but at times he seemed more mature than she thought. Seven years old, going on thirty. When Melissa caught herself really looking at her son, she didn't see much of herself in him.

He had her big brown eyes and light number of freckles, but that was pretty much it. His hair was so dark it almost looked black. His nose was not as petite as hers and he had a strong chin. He had a square shaped face compared to her oval shaped. When she really looked at him, she knew he looked like his father. It had taken her a while to look at him without the reminder of what she'd been through. But as the months went on and she watched her sweet baby grow, she realized that she couldn't hold what happened to her against him. She wouldn't be able to love him the way he deserved if she didn't let the anger and pain from the rape go.

So, with God's grace she was able to find a comfortable peace about it all. Not that she still didn't have moments where the evil pit would try to clench her ankles and suck her down, but she would look at those moments in faith. Faith that tomorrow will be a better day than yesterday. Finding a way to forgive a guy she didn't know for causing her to lose more than just her innocence. Then forgiving herself for the guilt and shame she placed on herself. Believing that in doing so she would become a better version of herself, not just for her own happiness, but that of her son's as well.

Wyatt shot a sideways glance at her and asked, "What?"

Melissa smiled and said, "Nothing. Just thinking how lucky I am to have you."

"Oh, Mom. Are you going to get mushy on me right now?" Wyatt picked up his clean plate and placed it in the sink.

Melissa stood and placed her plate in the sink with his, then grabbed him around the shoulders pulling him into a hug. "You bet." She kissed the top of his head and released him. Before too long he was going to outgrow her and have the upper hand. "I've got to get my hugs from you while I can. Love you."

Wyatt flashed her that boyish grin with cute dimples. "Love you too, Mom." His brown eyes were big and bright as he turned and ran back up the stairs. Julie and Gram returned through the back-patio door just as he disappeared.

"Hey sweetie, we were just reading the newspaper and finishing breakfast outside. Are you guys ready for the baseball game today?"

"Wyatt is for sure." Melissa loaded the dirty dishes into the dishwasher and turned it on. "Are you guys coming?"

Gram picked up her purse and slipped it over her shoulder. "Unfortunately, I have a doctor's appointment today and your mom volunteered to drive me."

"Not a problem. This is the last one for a little while since the holiday is coming up. The Lord knows I can use a break from baseball." She slid a few water bottles into her purse.

Gram leaned in and kissed her cheek. "You're such a good momma."

"Thank you, Gram. We'll see you later today then?"

Her mom guided Gram toward the front door. "We'll see you later. Good luck, Wyatt!"

Wyatt landed at the bottom of the stairs baseball cap on and equipment bag slung over his back. "Bye."

Melissa grabbed her keys off the hook. "Alright, Wyatt, are you ready to go?"

"Yep. I'm waiting on you." Wyatt bolted out the front door and laughed.

Melissa rolled her eyes and followed him out the door. She went to help him buckle his booster seat in, but he stopped her. "Mom, I can do it." Another reminder that he was growing up way too fast.

The drive there was full of Wyatt chatting on about his friends and about how he and James had worked really hard at practice. Melissa pulled into an empty spot to the south of the ball fields. Once she put the car in park, Wyatt was out the door and across the grass to the dugout where James and his team were getting ready. Melissa slowly followed behind carrying his equipment bag.

"Hey, Melissa." James relieved her of the bag.

Adjusting her purse, she gave him a casual smile. "Thanks. I still have to work on him about being responsible for his bag. He still thinks that's my job."

"I'll have a little chat with him. Cami's in the bleachers." James pointed toward the five tiered bleachers to the east of the field.

"Thanks." Melissa made her way to the bleachers and walked up toward Cami. "How are you?"

"Great! Jade had to run back to get her sunglasses out of her car. How are you?" Cami was upbeat as always.

"Alright. Wyatt is like a bull dozer everywhere he goes. I miss the days when he needed a nap in the afternoons." Melissa settled into her seat. "I've got to say I'm glad this is the last game for a while."

Cami clasped Melissa's hand. "You are a great, mommy. Kids are pretty much impossible to keep up with. Just wait until he can drive. Keep your head up."

"Thanks, Doctor Phil," Melissa said sarcastically.

"Is Cami giving advice again?" Jade joked as she walked up and took a seat on the other side of Melissa.

"Ha ha," Cami said. Then she shifted toward Melissa. "I need to let you know something."

"Ok. What is it?" Melissa asked and Jade leaned in to hear.

"James said Blake may come by the field today." Melissa's stomach dropped to her feet. Cami must've seen it on her face. "James is hanging out with him afterwards. As far as we know he still doesn't know about Wyatt. I thought you might've talked to him already. You haven't talked to him, have you?"

"No," Melissa breathed.

"I'm sorry. I guess James wasn't thinking when he ran into him."

"Thanks for telling me." Melissa dug for her sunglasses in her purse. It would be the best way to help hide her eyes from watching him just in case. Nothing. She remembered they were sitting on the counter and she didn't go back into the kitchen before leaving. She took a deep breath.

"Are you ok?" Jade leaned toward her and asked.

Melissa kept her eyes on the boys warming up. "Yeah, I'm fine."

Jade passed her a piece of gum. "I ran into him at the diner. I don't think you have to worry about him judging you, Mel."

Melissa looked at her friend and saw nothing but support in her eyes.

"I mean it. He still cares about you."

Melissa felt the tears spreading along the bottom rim of her eyes and she blinked rapidly to push them back. "I know I should've tried to meet him before now. I just kept running all the different ways the conversation would go in my mind."

Jade reached around Melissa and gave her a side hug. "The bright side, at least now he'll know."

That was true. She would just have to make it a point to have a conversation with Blake later when Wyatt wasn't around. There was no way she could avoid it now.

As the game began, she tried to put the thought of seeing Blake again out of her mind. She didn't want to keep over thinking it. Jade seemed to believe that Blake cared after her talk with him. Deep down Melissa hoped he truly did. She knew talking to him was inevitable. She just didn't think it would happen here, not with Wyatt present. She straightened her back and focused on the game.

All the boys did great. One by one they went up to bat. They tapped their bat on home plate and swung with all their hearts. Once the ball made contact with their bat they sprinted with all their might to first base. It was a joy to watch their teammates cheer and give hugs of encouragement through every hit and miss. James really had done a great job helping them learn sportsmanship and respect, along with their skills and positions. She felt like the innings were flying by. Wyatt didn't strike out once and assisted in five big outs as short stop.

It was the bottom of the last inning and Wyatt's team was in the lead. She cheered and enjoyed light conversation with Cami and Jade. The thought of Blake had all but left her mind, until she saw him.

******

Blake smiled as he walked up to the chain link fence next to the dugout and shook James' hand. "You look good out there, Coach."

"Thanks. I love these kids. This is the last inning and then we'll go grab lunch." James turned and took his place next to third base.

"Sounds good."

Blake watched James cheer on the next kid up to bat, number five. He was a pretty stocky kid and seemed tall compared to the others. Blake felt like the kid looked familiar for some reason but couldn't place it. On the third pitch, he hit it high into center field. The crowd cheered and the kid took off at a sprint. As he was rounding into second, James yelled for him to continue to third base. The ball was in the air as the kid paused on third base. He followed the ball as it hit the tip of the glove causing the baseman to stumble. The kid shot off the base as James cheered and pointed him to sprint for home. He slid into home plate just as the ball disappeared in a cloud of dust.

"SAFE!"

Number five's teammates started jumping up and down like they had just won the World Series. Blake laughed, remembering how big and important everything seemed as a kid. He had loved playing baseball and missed having that happy place to go to. The lessons he learned would always have an impact on his life: respect, discipline, passion, and teamwork. James gave the kid a high five. He saw number five turn and wave to someone in the crowd. It looked like he was waving to Cami, but then he recognized the two other women next to her. Jade and *Melissa*. Blake stood up straight. He looked at number five again and realized he knew where he'd seen the kid before. It was the kid who appeared to be living with Melissa.

"Number 5 is really good," Blake said to James as he walked back over to him. "He looks like he loves it."

James nodded his head. "Yeah. He loves to play. He's one that practices on his own like we used to, nonstop. The whole team is a good group of kids."

Blake smiled watching him head over to the dugout. "You're doing a great job."

"Thanks." James was called over by one of the parents. Blake stood back to wait until he was finished. His eyes made their way back to the stands, but they were empty. Then he noticed number five was in the dugout alone taking off his cleats.

Blake stepped just inside the door and said, "Hey, you were really good out there. My name's Blake Knoll. I'm a friend of James." He extended his hand.

"Thank you," he answered and shook Blake's hand. "James is family. Well, almost. He's marrying my aunt. I'm Wyatt. Wyatt Adair. See you later." Wyatt turned and left the dugout.

Adair? James is marrying his aunt?

Blake's mouth went dry as he struggled to swallow the lump in his throat. His eyes followed Wyatt as he made his way to the group of parents. When Melissa stepped away from the group, gave Wyatt a hug and he kissed her cheek. She looked up and met Blake's eyes.

Melissa's his mom?

Everything inside Blake stopped. She offered him a half smile and then turned to walk with Wyatt toward the parking lot. Blake stood there watching, frozen in time, as though at attention. It was like a shot from left field that he never saw coming. He had never considered Wyatt to be Melissa's son. His mind went wild thinking about her shutting him out completely and her family doing the same. Then Jade saying Melissa had been through so much. So, she found someone else? Wyatt had to be about seven. Did she cheat on him? His pulse hammered in his neck and he felt a panic rising.

"Are you going to stay in there all day?" James asked and leaned against the doorway.

Blake looked at James, not sure he had the ability to say anything. James must've seen it on his face. He looked back toward Melissa and Wyatt. "Wyatt's a good kid, great really."

"I didn't know..." Blake's voice trailed off still in shock. She didn't say anything to him about Wyatt and neither did anyone else. "She's a... mom?"

James's shoulders dropped. "Don't feel bad. There's no reason you would've known." He paused and looked back at Blake. "Melissa's an amazing mom."

"No one told me." Blake tried to hide the sadness in his voice.

"I'm sorry I didn't warn you. I didn't really know what to do. You're one of my oldest friends and I wanted to tell you but I care about Melissa's wishes too. She's been through a lot and it's not anyone's place to share that." James straightened his back. "Life has a way of ending up exactly the way it's supposed to even if the journey isn't what we expected."

Blake looked at James, but couldn't find any words. His eyes dropped to the dirt. He couldn't do this. Blake turned and headed straight for his truck. He saw Melissa was waiting while Wyatt put his bag in the back seat of her car. He paused at the front of his truck and watched them. Melissa smiled at something Wyatt must've said. Then she looked past Wyatt and locked eyes with Blake again. The happiness drained from her face. Blake's chest constricted and he had the sudden urge to run over and hold her in his arms. He didn't know anything about her situation or her at all, even more so than he thought.

"Melissa," Blake called to her and took steps toward her. He had to say something, anything. Once nearing the side of her car, she turned away from him. Blake was desperate and pleaded, "Melissa, please."

"Not here, Blake." She looked back up at him then at Wyatt in the back seat. Her eyes were wet with unshed tears. "I'll come find you."

Melissa looked broken and Blake had a sudden desire to fix whatever it was. There was a desperation in her eyes. Blake realized he needed to give her some more time. At least she said she would come to him. "Ok," he said and took a step back.

She broke eye contact, slipped into the driver's seat, and pulled out of the parking space. Blake's heart broke for her and for the relationship they once had as her taillights disappeared.

Chapter 9

A cool breeze swept down Shasten Lane, causing some loose strands of hair to brush across Melissa's face as she looked out from her seat at the edge of the back porch. She tucked them behind her ears and leaned back against one of the back-porch posts. The screen door opened and Gram walked out with two glasses in her hands. "Tea, dear?"

"Thank you, Gram." Melissa took a big drink and set the glass down. She pulled her legs against her chest and enclosed her arms around them in a comfortable hug. Gram took a seat in her rocker.

"Wyatt was so excited about his game this morning. He had to tell me all about it." Gram said, gliding back and forth in the rocker. "He's talking your mom's ear off now."

Melissa smiled up at her. "I'm glad." Wyatt was always so happy and warm with people.

"Is everything alright, Melissa?"

She took a deep breath. Gram was so discerning. "Is it that obvious?"

Gram smiled. "You've never been the best at hiding your emotions. You want to talk about it?"

Melissa loosened her arms around her legs. "Oh, I've just been thinking a lot," she said flatly.

"I see. Does it happen to have anything to do with a handsome young man who's moved back in across the street?"

Melissa leaned her head back against the post. There was no use trying to hide it from Gram. "I saw him at the coffee shop a little over a week ago. He actually approached me and we had a conversation." Gram remained silent. "I didn't tell him about Wyatt."

"Does he know?" Gram's voice was steady and comforting.

Nodding her head Melissa continued, "He does now. He found out about Wyatt when he saw me at the game today. He went to hang out with James afterward."

Nodding Gram asked, "So, what's the problem?"

Melissa struggled to find the words. "I just can't stop thinking about everything. About how we were before he left for basic, the rape, his unanswered letters, Wyatt, and now him being back here." She looked up at the blue sky. "I can't help but think about it and I don't know how I feel about it."

"Why didn't you tell him about Wyatt?"

Melissa traced the seam of her jeans. "I couldn't at first. Then I decided to just tell him I had a special little guy in my life and his phone rang. It was an important call and I let him leave." She knew he deserved answers. He had never done anything wrong when it came to them. But when she thought about saying anything to him regarding her rape and pushing him away, she couldn't find the words. So, she never walked across the street.

Gram looked north over the sunflowers. "The ghosts from our past have the ability to haunt not just our present but what we believe about our future."

Melissa thought about Gram's words. Her rape was something she'd been able to push to the back of her mind most days. It was always there, but she'd learned to cope better. She hadn't been able to sleep through her pregnancy. Horrible nightmares of her running from a nameless man made sleeping a fear. Her paranoia would often cripple her at the sound of anyone coming up behind her. If a guy tried to get close to her she would get a sick feeling in her stomach and panic would cause her to flee. She struggled with the thought of getting close to any man physically or emotionally.

Once she let her friends and family convince her it was time to try dating, Wyatt had started t-ball and she got busy. She could count on one hand the number of guys she had dated in the past eight years. It wasn't high on her priority list because she was just trying to be a mom, a single mom. Was she allowing her sole focus on Wyatt's wellbeing effect the way she viewed her future? Yes. She hadn't been thinking about her future at all. Wyatt's sure, but not her own. In a way, she thought she didn't deserve love at this stage in her life. She had only ever loved Blake and then gave it up.

The rocker came to a stop and Melissa looked up at Gram. "I've talked with Blake a few times. He seems at peace with a lot of things, but I have a hunch he still needs a safe place. He asked if he could visit the sunflowers."

"What?" Melissa hadn't expected him to go out there.

Gram looked at Melissa. "He takes a walk in there several times a week." She nodded toward the field and stood up from her chair. She kissed Melissa's forehead and then went inside leaving Melissa alone.

Melissa looked past the back yard out at the sunflowers. The old oak tree towered in the distance. She leaned her head against the post and closed her eyes. Blake had been walking through the sunflowers. Did he go to their spot? What if he was out there right now?

She thought about the pleading look in Blake's eyes after the baseball game. He wanted to talk to her. She told him she would come find him and now was the time. The conversation that had haunted her all these years was finally going to happen, as long as she kept her emotions under wraps. No matter what Blake's reaction, acceptance or judgement, she was going to face him like she should've eight years ago.

She pushed off her knees, stepped out onto the grass, and headed north toward the sunflowers.

******

Blake's shirt was drenched and it wasn't from his run that he chose to forgo tonight, he just didn't have it in him. Thank the Lord for a cool breeze to cut the Texas heat. The tips of his fingers traced the grooves on the root of Mrs. Meyers's old oak tree. After watching Melissa drive away, Blake drove back home needing to be alone. He stayed inside his living room, lights and TV off, just staring at the ceiling. His mind was a jumbled mess. It ranged from some brief clarity, to more confusion, and even more questions. Blake made a point to eat dinner quickly. His childhood home was never a place of happiness for him and even now he could feel the walls closing in on him. He had to escape and knew there was only one place to go when he felt like this. He leaned his head back against the oak's trunk and sighed.

When James had asked him to swing by the t-ball game, Blake never thought he would see Melissa. He had thought several times about approaching her in the afternoons when she was returning home with Wyatt from what he could assume was the summer youth program. But something inside him cemented his feet on his dad's driveway, never crossing the street.

Learning that Melissa was teaching and living in her grandmother's house was a surprise. But there was no way he could describe the shock that gripped him knowing that she had a son. In the military, he was trained to be prepared for anything and to be able to have the correct response. But this wasn't something he could have prepared himself for. As far as he could tell, the father wasn't involved or at least didn't come around much. If she was dating someone surely he would've seen them together at the house.

Just seeing her in the coffee shop brought back the tug-a-war of sorts in his heart. Should he keep holding onto hope that she'd come back to him or accept that she chose to end their relationship for good? He had always wanted to protect her and be there for her. He had promised he would. He hated the thought of her going through that alone. But he wasn't sure she would want him to extend a hand. She had chosen to remove him from her life and she probably still felt that way.

Releasing a long breath, Blake looked out at the sun inching closer to the top of the sunflowers. His eyes found Melissa's old home on the opposite side. His eyes rested on the third window from the right on the second floor. How he longed for the chance to reach into the nook and send her a signal to meet him. Why couldn't it be simple like it was when they were in high school? Their friendship was strong and they shared a special bond that was hard to replicate. He had tried to find a friend in the military or in dating, but none compared to Melissa. Like her house across the field, their relationship had changed and she had shared the most intimate part of herself with someone else. All that remained were shadows and memories of what used to be.

Blake was proud that they had chosen to remain abstinent while they dated. Melissa was raised in church and was strong in her convictions. Something that Blake didn't necessarily agree with at first, but luckily he hadn't been with anyone prior to Melissa. He had gone to church with her every Sunday at first as a way to simply get a break from his home. He hadn't agreed with everything the preacher said, but he wanted to be with Melissa and he respected her. When he enlisted, he told himself to keep that promise for her and he had. As the years went by and he tried accepting that she didn't want a relationship, he realized that he was proud of himself for keeping his promise. It changed from wanting to honor Melissa to honoring himself and Christ. His convictions had cost him on the relationship front, but he was ok with that.

He heard the stalks of the sunflowers shift and his back stiffened. The grass gave way to footsteps getting louder as they made their way toward him. Instincts kicking in, Blake slid his hands onto the ground beside him bracing to get up. Then the steps stopped. He pushed off the ground and saw just the girl he hoped it would be.

"Melissa," His voice evaporated as he said her name.

She stood before him fidgeting with the hem of her shirt. Her chocolate hair draped over her shoulders with a light glow from the setting sun behind her. She wore a purple flowing shirt, boot cut jeans, and sandals. It was like Blake blinked and they were in high school again. Her eyes slowly rose from her feet to meet his. They were full of remorse. Her cheeks flushed enhancing the freckles just below her big brown eyes. She sighed as she spoke. "Hi, Blake."

His pulse pounding in his throat, he strained to swallow. He waited for her to speak, hoping that she didn't feel he was invading her space. It was her grandma's field after all. "I'm sorry if I'm intruding."

"It's alright." She shifted her weight and took a deep breath. "Gram told me you'd been coming out here a lot. I think it makes her happy that you do."

"Yeah. I'm thankful for that." Blake motioned to the field. "It's still the same."

Melissa nodded in agreement, then her shoulders fell as she exhaled. "I didn't know you even remembered this spot was still here." Her eyes surveyed the opening around them.

Blake followed her line of sight and smiled. "It's probably the safest place in the world for me. How could I forget about it?"

She stared at him for a minute and he knew she was remembering just like him. It had been that for both of them. She dropped her hands to her sides.

"Blake, I've been meaning to talk to you since seeing you at the coffee shop that day." He could see the emotion swirling in her eyes. "I didn't know you would be at the game this morning. That's not how I wanted you to find out about Wyatt." She dropped her eyes to the ground.

Blake said nothing because he didn't trust that his hurt, confused, and frustrated response would achieve what he wanted.

Meeting his eyes again she continued, "I'm sorry I didn't tell you about him sooner. A lot has happened and it's not an easy thing for me to talk about."

Blake's shoulders remained tense. They shared a couple silent seconds. Melissa wrung her hands and her eyes darted past him toward the pond. She tucked a loose hair behind her ear. Blake was nervous to find out what but was desperate for it just the same. He hated seeing her like that.

"Blake, I can't..." her voice caught in her throat. "I can't tell you how—"

"Melissa," Blake interrupted, raising his hand and then dropped it. "I'm not going to lie. I have questions, lots of them. I was devastated when you never responded to my letters. I'd hoped you would be there for graduation before I got shipped out. That's what made the distance easier, thinking I was going to see you soon. But none of that happened." He released a deep breath and continued. "I know you had your reasons. I had hoped that you'd one day understand you could talk to me about it. I'd hoped that you'd lo—" He caught himself from saying love. He was so sure that she had loved him, but he wasn't sure he was ready to find out if that was true. The last thing he wanted was to push her away. He needed to have patience and let her tell him. "I hope you will, but I don't want you to share until you're ready."

She dropped her eyes and Blake saw the tears running down her face. Her emotion had him wanting to ask more questions. He wanted to touch her and hold her. He wanted her to know that he cared and was there for her. Without worrying about her stopping him, Blake closed the distance between them and slid his hands around her face. Her hot tears pooled on his thumbs. Blake stared into her chocolate brown eyes willing her to believe that he didn't want her to push him away. He saw reluctance, sadness, and possibly longing looking back at him. She was guarded and didn't seem ready to fully let him in. He kissed her forehead, lingering while he breathed in the smell of her hair and felt the warmth of his skin. To his relief, she didn't push him away. He stepped back and slid his hands in his pockets to give her some space.

She wiped her face and took some staggered breaths. "I want to tell you. I've always wanted to tell you, but didn't know how."

"I believe you." He saw what he thought was surprise in her expression.

"You do?" Her voice soft.

He nodded. "I do."

She pressed her lips tightly and he could see her eyes filling with water again. "I never thought you would be so kind or understanding to me and you don't even know what happened yet."

That broke his heart. "I don't want to be the cause of any more pain for you, Melissa. I've waited eight years; I can wait a little while longer."

Her face relaxed and she nodded. "Thank you for saying that. Only a few people know all the details." Her inhale was staggered. He was worried that it was worse than he originally thought. Then she said something that melted his heart. "I need you to know that I've only ever truly loved one person. You."

Blake felt like his heart would explode out of his chest. Hope burst through every fiber of his body. Then the pounding beat of his heart halted. *Loved? Past tense.* He knew she loved him when he left but what about now? Would it be possible for her to still love him? If not, could she learn to love him again? All he could do was stare at her as his mind jumbled with even more questions.

"I'm sorry, Blake." Melissa looked up at the sky and closed her eyes. "I know I sound like a broken record. There's so much I want to say, I just don't know how." Her face shifted so something scared and she turned toward the sunflowers. "I'm not sure I can do it now."

He panicked that she was fleeing and it shocked his body awake. Even if she wasn't ready to tell him what happened he couldn't let her leave without saying one more thing. "Melissa," Blake called just as she reached the sunflowers and he ran to catch up to her. She looked over her shoulder and then turned to face him. He engulfed her in a hug. The tension in her body slowly relaxed against him. She wrapped her arms around his waist. "I can't let you leave without telling you something." He leaned back to look into her eyes. "I'll wait. I'll wait as long as you need. Don't push me away again. I don't know if I can take it a second time."

She closed her eyes and nodded.

"I'm going to let you go now. But please, please come back to tell me." His voice a whisper as he pleaded with her.

"I will."

He was going to give her some more time. He hoped she would think about what he'd just said to her tonight. He leaned down and kissed her cheek. "Good night, Mel."

"Good night, Blake." Then she disappeared beyond the stalks.

Blake dropped his head. He dug his heels into the soil. He was going to give her some time. He wasn't positive what his timeline was, but he knew he had to wait it out for Melissa, no matter the cost.

Chapter 10

Melissa hurried down the sidewalk hoping she wouldn't be too late. There was a parent that stayed a little longer than she thought after the tutoring session that afternoon. She wasn't one to brush a parent off but she had received a voicemail from Mrs. Hall, the editor of Shaw Creek Press about a special article she wanted Melissa to take on. She rounded the corner and rushed in the front door.

Mary, the front desk attendant, greeted her. "Good afternoon, Melissa. Please go on back, Mrs. Hall is expecting you."

Melissa took a handful of steps and was at Mrs. Hall's office door. She waved Melissa in as she was wrapping up a call. The office was simple but very busy. Melissa paused just inside the door. The desk was organized with very little clutter and multicolor sticky notes marking various pages stacked to the side. Mrs. Hall replaced the phone on its base and Melissa stepped forward. "Sorry I'm late. I was worried I might've missed you."

"Not at all." Mrs. Hall motioned for Melissa to take a seat. "Where's Wyatt?"

"After tutoring I asked him if he wanted to come with me and he said no. Apparently, throwing a baseball in Gram's backyard was more fun." She chuckled. "So I dropped him off at home on my way here."

"He's a typical boy." Mrs. Hall smiled and then dove right into business. "You've done such a great job filling in for different columns this summer. Everyone loves your stories."

"Thank you. I've enjoyed writing." Melissa said, grateful for the compliment.

"I have a special story for you." Mrs. Hall pulled a file from her top desk drawer. "The 4th of July is next weekend. We are doing a 'Hometown Hero' article. We want to honor someone from Shaw Creek and let our community be able to give thanks for their service." She pulled out a couple of sheets. "We will run the article in next week's paper and then present the soldier with a commemorative plaque at the 4th of July festival."

Melissa was honored to be asked to take on such a special story. One of the nice things about Shaw Creek is they took care of their own and supported their military. "I'd be honored to do the story for you." She paused. "May I ask what made you pick me?"

Mrs. Hall paper clipped the pages and smiled. "Well, your grandmother is the one who submitted the soldier we chose."

Melissa's stomach tightened. There was only one soldier Gram would submit. Before she could respond, Mrs. Hall handed Melissa the pages. "Here you go. We want facts about his life but also to know if he is involved in the community." She stood up and extended her hand to Melissa. "You'll do great. Don't worry about your other column this week. We'll just fill it with something else. We've already contacted him to let him know he was selected. He is aware that the interviews will be taking place this week and someone will be contacting him to set up a time. Just have it submitted to me by Friday so we can run it on time."

"Thank you, Mrs. Hall." Melissa shook her hand and headed toward the exit. After saying good bye to Mary at the front desk, she pushed through the front door and started down the street back to her car.

She took a deep breath and looked down at the pages in her hand. At the top of the page was the traditional Shaw Creek Press Header and the first line under it read 'Our Hometown Hero'. Melissa's eyes made their way through the fine print regarding the article and she slowed to a stop when she saw the name and contact information for the chosen soldier. Blake Knoll. Just as she thought.

Of course, Gram submitted Blake for the story. She loved Blake and he'd helped her recently. She couldn't say no to the article now just because she had history with Blake. That's not the type of person she was, even though it would be the easier thing to do. After seeing Blake last night in the sunflower field, she had thought a lot about his response to her. He had been understanding and sympathetic. Her heart clinched at remembering the words he said to her. The longing look in his ocean blue eyes as he pleaded with her to not push him away. He was waiting for her to tell him everything.

She sighed and slipped the pages into her purse. He did say to not be a stranger. She guessed this article wasn't going to allow her to be one. What could it hurt? She could learn about his time in the service and about how it has impacted his life now. How hard could that be? She needed to set up a time to meet him after her tutoring class at the library. The positive thing was that she knew right where to find him.

Melissa parked her car and stepped out onto Gram's driveway. Across the street, the living room light was on and Blake's truck was backed in front of the garage. She took a deep breath and headed toward the inevitable. She stopped in front of his door and pulled out the pages from Mrs. Hall.

Ding Dong. No backing out now. After a moment Blake pulled open the door. "Melissa." He looked surprised.

"Hi, Blake." She gripped the papers a little harder. "I hope I'm not interrupting you."

"Not at all. Please come in." He stepped back to allow space for her to enter.

"Thank you, but this will only take a minute." She wasn't sure going inside was a good idea. At least not yet.

"Ok. Is Wyatt with you?" Blake looked past her.

"Um, no I dropped him off earlier so he could practice throwing his baseball." She motioned over her shoulder.

Blake smiled and nodded his head. "Good. He likes to practice, huh?"

"Yes, all the time." She paused. "I just have to let you know something."

"Ok." Blake raised his eye brows.

She looked down at the papers. "The Shaw Creek Press asked people to submit local soldiers for selection of our hometown hero. Mrs. Hall told me she has been in contact with you and let you know you'd been selected." She paused. "They have asked me to do the interview and article for next week's paper." She handed him one of the papers.

"Yes, she called me. I'm honored." He smiled at her. She loved his smile. "Did she say who submitted my name?"

Melissa pointed across the street. "Gram. She's very fond of you."

The left side of his mouth raised in a half smile as he looked over her shoulder. "And I'm very fond of her too." He looked back at the page.

Melissa pulled out her phone and opened her calendar. "I'm needing to schedule a time for the interview. It may take two meetings since I work at the library the rest of the week. Well, except on Thursday."

"I can meet any time after lunch pretty much every day." He dropped his hands down to his side. "Where would you like to meet?"

They needed somewhere neutral. "Let's start tomorrow and then go from there. Let's meet at the coffee shop say 3:00pm? The kids leave at 2:00pm, but I usually don't finish cleaning up until 2:30pm."

"Perfect."

Melissa set the alert in her phone, not that she was going to need the reminder. Like she could forget she was going to spend time with Blake. She slipped the paper back into her purse and then met his eyes again. "Great. I'll see you tomorrow then?"

"Yeah. Thanks for doing this, Melissa." He looked like he may reach for her and she wasn't so sure she'd stop him.

"Goodnight, Blake." She turned and walked back across the street. She retreated behind Gram's front door and leaned against it. *This won't be bad.* As long as she could keep things professional.

"You ok, Mom?" Wyatt asked.

She turned to see Wyatt sitting on the sofa with Gram. "Yeah. I just had a busy day. What are you watching?"

"The Lego Movie," he said turning back to the TV.

She pushed off the door. "I love that movie. Let me grab some popcorn. I'd love a date with my special guy."

Melissa ruffled his hair and she walked past him to the kitchen. She was going to need a moment to get her heart back down to a normal pace, especially if she was going to be spending more than a few minutes with Blake in the near future. Smiling to herself, Melissa couldn't help but look forward to it.

Chapter 11

Melissa sipped her hot tea as she reviewed the questions she had for Blake. She was surprisingly calm considering the butterflies that had been in her stomach all night. He seemed grateful last night when she told him about it. He'd done so much with his military service, why not honor Blake?

"Hey there." Melissa looked up to see Blake standing opposite of her. "May I join you?"

He was wearing jean shorts and a black t-shirt. Her eyes started to drift from his eyes toward his chest. He looked so good. She shook her head. *Focus.* She just needed to ask one question at a time and focus on the article.

"Yes. Of course, please sit." She pulled her papers close to her in a nice neat stack. Blake sat across from her. She pulled out her pen and adjusted the paper. "I have a list of questions, but we may venture off to others depending on how our conversation goes."

"Sounds good," Blake said nodding his head in understanding. He took a drink from his water bottle and smiled.

Reverting her eyes back to the papers, Melissa took a deep breath. The first question at the top of the list was one she already knew the answer to or so she thought. It would be best to ask anyway to make sure she was right. She took a deep breath. "I know the answer to this but I wanted to hear it from you. When did you join the military?"

Without hesitation Blake answered. "I enlisted in the fall of my senior year in high school. It was in early October if I remember correctly. I was 18." He took another drink and then continued. "I went to basic training the following fall, in August." His tone was warm and didn't seem uneasy at all. She hoped that she was giving him the same impression.

Melissa finished taking her notes. *That wasn't so hard.* She went to the next question. "I know you chose the Marine Corps. Why did you decide to enlist and what made you choose that branch?"

When she looked up at him she saw tension in his face. He looked down at his water bottle tapping his thumb on the laminate table top like he was debating what to say. This question brought her back to the past. The struggles Blake had gone through were horrible and she had done her best to help him out of that. Now that the question was out, she regretted asking it, for bringing it up. She had pushed those memories far away. She had stored in the deepest cavern in her heart in hopes of not having to revisit it ever. It appeared that Blake was struggling with the same thing.

"Blake, I'm sorry. It's just one of the questions—"

"It's ok. I figured they'd want to know." He looked up at her and the tension in his face had softened some. "I wasn't the best student in high school. I was better at sports than school work. My family life was rough and I had no money for college." He took a deep breath. "I had someone counting on me and I couldn't let her down. I had to make something of myself, given that I didn't have much support at home."

Melissa could feel the emotion building in her chest. She began writing again so she didn't have to look in his eyes.

Blake continued, "I was young and desperate. I didn't believe there was any other way to get educated at the time. So, I went to the recruiting offices in Dallas. I did my research before going and believed that the Marines had a broad range of opportunities and that it was the best fit. After visiting with their recruiting officer, I was sold. It's hard to explain but I just felt at peace about it."

They looked at each other for several silent beats. She swallowed knowing that there might be more to the story but let it go. She blinked and looked back down at her paper, pausing before writing. She didn't have time to worry about that right now. She quickly wrote down notes to summarize what he said.

"Can I say something?" Blake's voice caught her off guard. "Off the record if you don't mind."

"Ok." She leaned back letting her back settle into the curve of the chair.

"Please don't apologize for asking me questions about that. We're friends and I'm ok talking about it with you." His voice was sincere and familiar. "I'll always answer your questions."

"We're really friends?" She said breathlessly. It had been a long time since she used the word 'friends' to describe their current relationship.

"Of course. I view you as friend, always will." Blake reached out and placed his hand over hers. His touch was tender and she missed knowing what that felt like.

"Melissa?" Blake asked softly. Her eyes moved to look at him knowing he would see the emotion there. "I want to have a comfortable relationship with you. One where we can share freely and trust that we will respect each other."

She nodded and looked down at their hands. Guilt. She knew that she was the one causing this strain. "Ok."

Blake gave her hand a light squeeze and then pulled away. "Good, because I'd hate to think the next few days are going to be uncomfortable." He offered her his country boy smile.

"I'm sorry. I guess I didn't know what to expect from this."

"It's just me, Melissa. Let's both try to have no expectations. Sound good?"

"Sure." She cleared her throat. "Next question: What did you do in the Marines?"

She sat back in her seat and took a sip of her tea. This was something she knew nothing about.

Blake answered, "I was a Marine Raider. It's special forces." He smiled back at her, his eyes full of pride. "It was one of the greatest things I've ever done."

"Special forces? Sounds important. What did it entail?"

She tried not to notice the flex in his shoulders as he leaned forward and placed his elbows on the table. "Well, it's a lot of training. More than I really expected. There was a grueling physical side that took months to achieve the peak level of skill. Then the mental side. It took a lot to train my mind to block out emotions and focus on the task at hand. We had to maintain our training to be ready at any moment. We never knew what the next mission might be so we had to be prepared for every scenario."

Melissa paused and looked up at him. He was looking out the window as he spoke.

"I've seen the best in people and the worst in people, the very worst. I've seen things like people sacrificing themselves, their wives, or their children for evil acts. They attack their own people just to prove a point and don't care what it takes to do it." Blake's voice trailed off for a moment. Melissa studied Blake's face but it was unreadable. Then he looked back at her and continued. "So, it's not always been easy, but it made me have to look at life through a different lens. The guy next to me needed me to be in top form, physically, emotionally, and mentally so that we both came home. I value things differently and remember those who didn't make it back."

"I can't even imagine." Melissa knew she couldn't sympathize with Blake about what he'd seen and experienced. There was no way she could understand. "It sounds like a huge commitment."

"It was." He took a drink. "After three years in the Marines I did a lot of different qualifying exercises and my superiors suggested special ops. After a lot of thinking I wanted to give it a try. It would give me advanced skills and the opportunity to serve my country in a way very few people do. I wasn't sure I could do it, but I figured I didn't have anything to lose. It was something that just fit for me. We developed skills such as navigation, demolitions, and marksmanship. We had to be individually strong in order to connect as a team. And we were a very strong team. They were the best." He paused. "I'd do it again in a heartbeat."

His last statement made her heart ache just a little. Doing it again meant leaving again. She returned his smile then looked for the next question. "Where were you stationed during your time in the Marines?"

He rubbed his hands on his thighs. "Well, before I joined the Raiders, I spent time in Georgia. Then I went to North Carolina for special training."

She wrote his answer then looked up. "How was that?"

"It was tough, really tough. I've heard people say to 'give it all you got' no matter what it is. Well, I didn't fully understand what that meant until I went to training. All the things I mentioned before, we had to develop and prove we were skilled in."

"Where did you go after training?" Melissa kept writing as fast as she could.

"Germany."

She looked up and raised her eyebrows. "Europe. Really?"

"You sound surprised." Blake said through his smirk.

"I don't know much about how the military moves you guys around." She should've known all of this. They were supposed to have a happily ever after and they would've been able to experience these things together. He wouldn't have had to been alone.

He took another drink from his water bottle. "I understand that. Most of our missions were done in the Middle East. I spent most of my time out there. I've been a lot of places and like I said before it's not always been with the best of people." His blue eyes turned a dark grey and his face flashed something she couldn't place.

Melissa worried about how much his service had really affected him. What had he seen? What did he struggle with? She wasn't sure she was ready to know any more about that last question. She finished taking her notes and then placed her papers into a nice neat stack.

"Well, I think that's a good place to start. I'm sure Mrs. Hall told you she would like information about what you do for the community and then an interview with your dad if he's willing. I know you may not have anything as far as community may go." Her phone chimed as a text message came in. She smiled when she saw it was from Gram but written by Wyatt.

"What is it?" Blake asked.

"Oh, it's Wyatt. Gram lets him text me on her phone. He said he got his math tutoring worksheets done and was ready for me to come home. He's ready to practice his batting. I'm the pitcher. After tutoring we usually practice at the park or in the back yard. Since I'm with you, he's making sure I don't forget. And he's reminding me about the aquarium show this weekend. He thinks I won't remember anything." She texted him back that she'd be there that afternoon. She laid her phone down and went back to the papers. "Ok. Do you think your dad would be ok with me visiting with him?"

When Blake didn't say anything, she looked up. His eyes were tender and so familiar transporting her to what seemed like another lifetime. Confused she asked, "What?"

He slightly shook his head, "I was just thinking about how amazing you are. I didn't know if anyone has told you that lately."

Heat began to rush up her chest to under her jaw. Her voice seemed to disappear and she was frozen to the wooden seat under her jeans. Some compliments tended to make her uncomfortable because she didn't always think of herself as worth the attention. Perhaps it's because the compliment was from him, the only person she had loved hearing them from. She managed to say, "Thank you."

They stared at each other for what seemed like an eternity. She wanted so badly to see inside his head. What was really going on underneath? No matter how long it had been, Blake still had a special pull in her heart.

His voice suddenly broke her trance. "I'll talk to dad but I don't think it will be a problem. For the community part, I've been helping wounded vets with physical therapy at the V.A. hospital. We could start there. Then do the last part at the cancer center with dad."

Gaining her bearings again she said, "Sounds good. When are you going there next? Can I tag along with you?"

"Actually, I'm free if you'd like to go now?"

"Oh, great. Let me text Gram and tell Wyatt I'll be another couple of hours." She pulled out her phone and sent the message really quick.

He stood and turned to leave. "Do you want to ride together? It's about a thirty-minute drive with traffic."

Melissa hesitated for a second. "That's ok. I'll just drive myself. Since I'm already postponing with Wyatt it will take longer if we have to come back for my car. Let's meet in the front lobby."

She thought she saw a bit of disappointment flash across his face and then it was gone. "Ok." He turned to leave then paused and looked over his shoulder. "Thanks for doing this interview, Melissa. I'll see you in just a bit." Then he turned and headed out the door.

She grabbed her folder and made her way out to her car. *That wasn't so bad.* It was easier than she thought it would be. Blake was respectful and honest. She gripped the laced leather of her steering wheel soaking up its heat through her fingers.

When he said they were friends and he would always be honest with her she felt guilty. Even though he knew she wasn't ready to tell him about her rape, she still felt horrible about making him wait. She had only meant to take a week at most to tell him. Then she was chosen to do this article. Their time together was going smoothly, so far. In fact, she was glad to be doing it. She was nervous at first but once they got to talking she was happy to hear about his life after high school.

Everything he'd told her in the sunflower field had given her hope in the possibility that he wouldn't reject her. If she told him about her rape and why she didn't give him the chance to understand, she feared their friendship would be completely ruined. He was a big part of her life and she knew it had been the biggest mistake of her life to throw that away. This time it wouldn't be because of her choice but his.

Chapter 12

Blake slid out of his truck and zig zagged through the parking lot of the V.A. hospital. As one of five cancer centers in the Dallas area, the place was typically busy. He held open one of the heavy glass doors for an elderly couple and then slipped behind them into the lobby. The clean white tile and large windows lit up the space. He took the only open seat to the right of the doors and watched for Melissa.

"Blake!" He turned to see the VA director approaching him. The director extended his hand with a smile.

Blake stood to meet him and shook his hand. "Good morning, Mr. Roberts. No, I'm not volunteering today. I've been chosen by the Shaw Creek Press as their hometown hero for the 4th of July. They wanted to interview me regarding my volunteer work at the VA. I'm waiting to meet their journalist right now."

"Why that's great! I will let the rehab unit know that you're going to be coming up. Then you won't have anyone ask questions about the extra person." Mr. Roberts pulled out his pager.

"I appreciate it, sir. We should just be a few hours."

"Not a problem. We love to have people share what we do here in the V.A." He paused. "Blake, I know you don't know for sure what your plans are but I wanted to ask you about possibly coming on full time here at the center. You do a great job and everyone has such high praise for you. We'd pay for your training and certification."

Blake felt completely blown away. Now he had two possible job opportunities. Both were helping veterans. "Sir, I don't know what to say."

"Don't feel any rush. I just wanted to mention it to you and maybe have a discussion at length about it with you in the future. You do a great job up there and I would love to have you here every day."

"Thank you, sir."

Mr. Roberts reached into his jacket and pulled some small papers out of his pocket. "I also want to give you these Wranglers tickets. The center was given several tickets to honor service members during the upcoming holiday. Would you like some?" He handed the tickets to Blake.

"Thank you. I really appreciate it." Blake took the tickets.

"Well, I've got to get to a meeting. See you later." They shook hands again and he was gone.

Blake slid the tickets into his wallet and returned to his seat. The air was filled with soft conversations and the ringing of phones. This place was amazing to Blake. Just seeing the number of people coming and going made him incredibly proud to be a veteran. So many people have given so much by serving their country and this was one place where he could get a chance to see some of them.

"Hey, Blake." Melissa's voice made him hop up quickly. She shot him a smile and said, "You looked like you were in a daze. Is everything ok?"

Man, she was so beautiful. Her hair fell over her shoulders with a light curl. Her green and pink floral blouse brought out a hint of green in her brown eyes, which he had noticed at the coffee shop but now as she stood on the white tile in the sunlight from the large windows, she took his breath away. It was like seeing her for the first time all over again, and it had only been about thirty minutes.

"Oh yeah. I was just watching everything going on around me." He guided her toward the elevators. "We need to go to Unit 16."

"This is a beautiful place. I've never been here before." Her eyes soaked up every detail around the room. "There's so many people."

He pushed the elevator button. "Yeah. It's a great thing to see so many people, who've served their country, have the opportunity to get health care." They entered the elevator and he pushed the button for floor three. Melissa's arm brushed against his as she stood next to him. He loved the feeling.

"So is there anything I should know before going in here for the first time?" Melissa looked up at him and once again he lost the air in his lungs. *She is amazing.* She must've noticed him staring because her eyes dropped to his mouth. When her eyes met his again the corners of her mouth crept up into a grin.

Blake cleared his throat. "Just stay with me and you'll be fine. These patients may have lost a part of themselves, but they are the hardest working and most friendly bunch you'll ever meet." The elevator door opened for them and he extended his arm. "After you."

As they exited the elevators, he watched her take everything in. The writer in her was always observing every detail around her. It was like she was putting it to memory so not to ever forget it. "The whole floor is for physical therapy," he said. She followed him to the check in desk. He pulled out his ID card and showed it to the attendant.

"Do I need to do anything?" Melissa said looking at his ID card.

"No. I took care of it already." He handed her a visitor badge. "Just wear this so they know you've checked in."

Melissa looked around the open room filled with equipment and specific stations to help people work toward recovery. "What do we do?" She turned to face him.

"Let's sit over here and I will answer some of your questions and then you can meet some of the veterans I get to help." He motioned her over to the row of chairs lining the outside wall. They settled into their seats and she pulled out her notepad and folder.

"Ok. This is a truly amazing place, Blake." She looked up and smiled. "What made you want to volunteer here?"

He looked out at the open room full of machines and patients. "I've been thinking about working with veterans for a while. So, when dad's doctor mentioned it to me it was really a no brainer." He paused trying to find the words to explain it. "I was lucky with all the missions I went on and all the difficult things I had to face. I never got hurt. I know several people who were not as lucky." A chair got pushed against a wall and made him flinch. He heard the shouts. He could taste the dust. Mangled pieces of metal appeared behind the smoke. Blake shook his head wishing the horrible memories away. He looked back at her and saw the hint of concern in her eyes. He hated anyone to see him when he had flashbacks.

She broke eye contact and wrote his answer before looking back out at the room. "This place is inspiring and yet I can't help but feel sad too."

"Yeah, I get that," Blake said with a nod. He definitely got that.

"Can I ask you a personal question?" Her voice was soft and seemed nervous.

Blake turned to look at her, but she kept looking forward. She had been given a glimpse of the nightmares he sometimes had, of course she'd want to ask a question. "Always."

She looked up at him and he could tell she was touched by his response. "Are you really ok?" her voice faded off.

His chest lifted and fell with the weight of a house. He didn't talk a lot about what he'd seen or been through. But he wanted to be honest with Melissa. She might not be able to be honest with him just yet, but he would always be with her. "There are lots of things I've seen. Things I will never be able to forget. Things that I wouldn't wish on my worst enemy. No matter what I went through before going on missions, nothing could've prepared me for all the evil, anger, pain, and death." His Adams apple bobbed as he swallowed. "Things I've seen. Things I've done. It's not always easy to accept but there's only one thing that's helped me. Prayer."

She tilted her head at him. "What do you mean?"

He felt himself slipping back to a dark place. A place he never wanted to return, but couldn't help sometimes. "Before I left for the military I can honestly say that I wasn't that religious. As I'm sure you remember. My home life was hard and the things that went along with that made me angry at God. I often felt like I had to manage on my own just to survive."

"I never wanted you to be alone through that." Her voice was soft and sad.

"I know. But there were times, dark times, that I didn't have a choice but to deal with it alone."

She looked down at her note pad and Blake placed his hand over hers. "Melissa, look at me." She did. "Don't feel bad. It was part of my past and I've dealt with it. Do I struggle sometimes? Yes. It's been more difficult coming home to be with dad. You were a great friend to me and I could never repay you for that."

She nodded slightly and took a deep breath. Blake knew he needed to get back to the interview for both their sakes.

"When I finished my Raiders training and started going on missions, I depended on myself to do things. I had to be there for my men and also for those I was trying to protect or rescue." He closed his eyes trying to shake the visions that were fighting for a place in the front of his mind. He took a deep breath and continued. "It's like with all the best training in the world, there still came a time when I faced failure. Depending on myself alone wasn't enough."

He could feel Melissa watching him and cleared his throat to continue. "After that I hit rock bottom. I pulled away from everyone, even my team. There were times I struggled with what my purpose was. Why did I survive and my friend did not? I realized that I needed help and it wasn't just from my brothers. I remembered coming to church with you and feeling like I didn't belong there. But at the same time, I felt like I needed to be there. So, I visited with the chaplain and he really cleared things up for me. He helped me understand what true salvation meant and how to have real faith with the things I can't control. I know I'm not perfect and I still mess up. But now I feel like the load I was carrying from my past, from my time serving, and what I hoped for the future is gone." He rung his hands together. "So in order to keep all those horrible memories, nightmares, and regrets from taking ahold of my heart, I have to pray, a lot. I believe they don't define me, God does. I cling to that truth and move past it."

Melissa's hand lightly landed on his forearm. He looked up at her and saw a warmth in her eyes. She smiled and said, "Thank you for sharing that with me."

"Thanks for listening."

She nodded. "Always."

Blake looked down at her hand and slowly took it in his. Her hand was soft and delicate just like he remembered. He wrapped his fingers around hers and lifted them to his lips. He closed his eyes and took in the feel of her soft skin on his lips. He returned their hands back to his thigh. "I want you to be a part of this side of my life. It's not always good, but I'm not going to hide that from you."

Blake couldn't place the look in her eyes and it scared him to think that he'd caused a reason for her to not want to be close to him. Blake's eyes dropped to her lips. Slowly, he leaned in toward her. Her lips parted and she took a deep breath. "Blake…"

He froze millimeters above her lips.

Chapter 13

Melissa held her breath. Blake pulled away from her and sat back against his chair. The desire in his eyes had vanished and was replaced with confusion.

"Blake, you don't want to kiss me."

"I don't?" he asked.

"I still haven't told you what happened. I'm not sure you'll think it's worth it after I tell you what happened and why I…" Her voice caught. "I don't want to ruin our time together while we do the article. I promise I'll tell you once this is done."

He stared at her for several beats. He bit the inside of his cheek and nodded. She wanted to kiss him, but was afraid that once that door opened they couldn't go back. Then it would hurt worse if he wasn't ok with what had happened. Melissa felt horrible. She realized she wasn't being fair or reasonable. He was telling her about the dark places in his mind and she still hadn't done it for him.

Blake had just bared his soul to her, honestly, openly, and without reservation. She knew there was no way that she could understand what he had gone through. If only she'd been there for him and not given up on them, regardless of her reasoning. Her heart broke at the thought of him going through all that alone. Before she'd thought about what she was doing she reached out and touched his arm. She meant it for comfort and to let him know that she cared. Then he kissed her fingers. She could still feel the tingle from where his lips had been. She curled her fingers around the edge of her notebook trying to calm the beautiful sensation his kiss gave her. She cleared her throat and realized she needed to get back to the task at hand.

"Um. Can you take me around and show me more about what they do in here?" She couldn't bring herself to look at him.

"Sure. I have several people I'd like to have you meet."

She stood and said, "You lead the way."

The next two hours seemed to fly by. She had never heard from such brave and inspiring people. All the therapists and assistants were gracious and loving to everyone there, including her. They all had struggles both physical and emotional, but listening to them made her feel like she was able to give them a hand in their recovery. Most of them were willing to talk to her and just gushed about Blake. Watching Blake laugh and love on these people made her heart melt. He had always been one to try and help others. Starting with his mom as a boy, to her as a young man, and now to his fellow soldiers as their brother. It was no surprise to her that he volunteered here. He couldn't do a lot of the hands-on things because he wasn't certified, but he encouraged and got whatever they might need. He was a great cheerleader as they struggled to complete different tasks. He was great at it. Tender and sympathetic to their struggles, yet he pushed them to be their best. He was helping them believe they could do all they dreamed of doing.

She was silent in the elevator ride back down to the first floor. Her mind was all over the place. She was trying to push back the personal longing to be close to him, to kiss him. She felt drawn to him like never before. *That's not what this is about.* She had to get through the article first. He still didn't know the truth. She couldn't give way to the possibility of getting close to him again when he may not want anything to do with her once he knew her secret.

Her cell phone dinged signaling a text message interrupting the conversation she was having in her head.

Cami: Hey girl. Sorry but I couldn't get tickets for the aquarium show. They already sold out.

Blake followed her out into the lobby. "Is everything ok?"

She looked up at him. "Yeah. I was going to take Wyatt to a show at the aquarium this weekend but they already sold out." She slid her phone back into her purse. "He's going to be bummed for sure."

"Hey, I was given some tickets to the Wranglers game this weekend. I know Wyatt likes baseball. You guys are welcome to join me. You know, as my friends."

An invitation from Blake? It had been a long time since they'd gone anywhere together. Would he consider this a date? Well, it wouldn't be a date because Wyatt would be there. He really would like to go to a Wranglers game. He loved them. Melissa and Blake were friends, old friends. She could feel the nervousness in her shoulders. Hesitant she responded, "Thanks for the offer. I don't know…"

"Oh come on, Melissa. I hate to think Wyatt is not getting to do something fun this weekend. At least think about it?"

Blake was right. Wyatt would prefer the baseball game over the aquarium anyway. She sighed and let her shoulders relax. "I'll think about it. Thanks for asking." She could see the slightest hint of disappointment in his eyes. She quickly changed the subject. "I would love to visit with your dad tomorrow. The newspaper loves to hear from family members."

"Sure. Dad would really like it."

"Great. I'll have to take Wyatt home first. Would 3:00pm be ok?"

"That'll be great. I'll meet you in front of the cancer center."

"Perfect. Thanks for showing me around today. I really loved it. You're doing something really amazing for them."

Once again he gave her his signature smile, the one that made her knees want to buckle.

"You're welcome. Thanks for coming." He paused as if he might say something else. "I'll see you tomorrow." He headed out the front door.

Melissa watched him walk away. She thought about the feel of his warm lips on her fingers and warmth of his breath as he hovered over her lips. *Man, I've got to stop thinking so much.* Knowing herself, it's not likely.

Melissa walked in the front door of Gram's and laid her bag down on the table and made her way toward the living room where her mom was reading a book, Gram was crocheting, and Wyatt was watching a movie. She smiled as she leaned against the door frame. She loved her family and wouldn't trade them for anything.

Gram looked up and smiled at her. "How was your day, sweetie?"

"It was good, really productive. I'm going to get a drink. Does anyone need anything?"

Wyatt shook his head no and Julie said, "No thanks."

Gram pushed off the sofa and straightened her back. "I'll join you."

Melissa retrieved two glasses from the cupboard. "Want some tea?"

"Sure," Gram sat at the table.

Melissa brought the two filled tea glasses and took a seat next to Gram. Like always, Gram's sweet tea hit the spot. Washing down her throat and cooling her nerves from the still lingering invitation from Blake. She hadn't stopped thinking about it since she left the V.A. hospital. The tug-of-war between guarding herself and doing what she wanted to do was threatening to rip her heart in two. She took another drink and closed her eyes.

"Is something on your mind, dear?" Grams voice broke through her thoughts.

"I'm really not good at hiding my feelings." Melissa smiled knowing there was no need to keep silent.

Gram smiled and placed her arm on Melissa's. "Let's talk about it."

Melissa sighed. "Well, you know I went and met with Blake today?"

Gram nodded but remained silent waiting for her to continue.

"Cami told me that she wasn't able to get tickets to the aquarium this weekend. I mentioned it to Blake while I was texting her back." Dropping her eyes to her tea glass she continued, "He invited us to go to the Wranglers game with him. Me and Wyatt."

"That was nice of him. What did you say?" Grams voice was genuine like always.

"I told him I'd think about it." Melissa looked up at Gram who had a tender smile creasing her wrinkled cheeks.

Curious Melissa asked, "What?"

"Why not go with him?"

"I don't know." Melissa looked out the window. "Is it a date?"

"Did he say it was?"

Keeping her eyes out the window. "He said we'd go as friends."

Gram paused for a moment. "I don't think it's a date. He invited Wyatt too. Could he just be doing something nice for an old friend?"

Dropping her eyes again to the ice cubes in the remaining tea. "Yes."

"So what's the problem?"

Melissa was hesitant to actually admit what she was trying so hard to push down in her heart. "I'm afraid to admit what I really want from him."

Gram's weathered hand pressed into Melissa smooth palms. "Just because your life took a different path doesn't mean you're supposed to live the rest of that beautiful life alone."

Melissa could feel the rims of her eyes filling with tears as she fought to hold them back.

Gram continued, "You're a single mother not a woman unworthy of love. You are allowed to feel things and find love." She lifted Melissa's chin to meet her eyes and her face was full of love and understanding.

Melissa suddenly felt the tears run down her face. The truth of Gram's words penetrated her heart. "I don't know how. I've been used and thrown aside without a thought. I don't see myself as someone worth loving."

Gram wiped her thumbs across Melissa's cheeks and held her face. "My sweet child, you are most definitely someone worth loving. I don't ever want to hear you say that again. Just because one man did that in your past doesn't mean they all will. Spending time with someone who was a really good friend to you is nothing to worry about." She dropped her hands onto Melissa's. "I say go. Wyatt would have a great time. Start by opening your heart up to friendship. You aren't meant to live in a bubble trapped by guilt or worry."

Melissa was hesitant, but understood Gram's point. It couldn't hurt anything to go. Besides Blake didn't have any family to take so why not take friends. Wyatt would have a blast and he may not be the only one.

Chapter 14

Blake's dad laid completely still in his hospital bed. The cool white sheets draped over his body and his arms resting at his sides. For a while Blake simply watched the rise and fall of his dad's chest. His skin was pale and face sunk in, exposing his once strong cheek bones. His dad was still getting some chemo treatment, but there was no proof of it helping. When Blake was at the center he mostly sat next to his dad while he slept. The hard heart he once had against his dad was beginning to break.

At one time, he could only bring himself to pity the man laying before him but now he genuinely felt sad. Watching his dad's health rapidly decline since being back ripped at Blake's soul. He wouldn't wish this on his worst enemy. Suddenly his dad's eyes struggled to open and he blinked trying to gain focus.

Blake leaned toward his dad and said, "Hey, Dad."

A weak smile spread across his dad's face as he turned to see Blake. His voice was raspy and weak, "Blake."

"How are you today?" Blake tried to maintain control of his worried voice.

"I'm awake so it's a beautiful day." His dad's voice was groggy and shook some. Suddenly Blake thought it might not be a good idea for Melissa to come today. In theory, it was a good idea but he didn't know if his dad could handle it.

"I need to ask you something, Dad."

Mr. Knoll's eyes remained focused on Blake, though he didn't say anything.

"You know the interview I'm doing for the 'Hometown Hero'?" His dad nodded and so he continued, "Well, Melissa is doing it and wanted to come and talk with you about having a son in the military. She was planning on coming this afternoon. Would you want to do that? If not, it's ok. I don't want it to cause more of a problem for you."

Mr. Knoll managed to adjust himself in his bed so he could be face to face with Blake. He took a deep breath and spoke. "Blake, I would love to talk with her."

"Are you sure?"

His dad smiled again and nodded. "Yes. I know I might not be the best father to talk about when you joined or why you served, but regarding who it has made you, that I can speak to."

All Blake could do was nod. He would go ahead and have Melissa come even if it might not be a long interview. This was all the family he had and if he wanted to share something then Blake would make sure he did. "Ok, dad. But I need to ask you something. It's very important that you listen to me and do as I ask."

"Yeah, son?"

"I can't have you bringing up your threats to Melissa. I don't want her knowing about your manipulation of me and your desire to cause her harm. To my knowledge she doesn't know anything about it. I was never going to tell her. She didn't need to worry about that and doesn't need that mess inhabiting any place in her life now. Understood?"

Mr. Knoll's face dropped. "I understand."

"Promise me you won't, Dad." Blake's voice was firm.

"I promise." He looked up at the ceiling. "You know I don't feel that way now, right? I was messed up—"

"Not now, Dad." Blake cut him off. "We're not going there right now. Just remember for when Melissa arrives."

Mr. Knoll nodded.

Blake turned on the TV and switched it over to the sports channel. He hated bringing up the past, especially when it involved his dad and Melissa. Settling back into his seat he pushed his anger inside and cleared his throat. He didn't want to spend any of his dad's time that he had left angry with him. He looked over at his dad and realized that he was given the opportunity to make up for lost time. Even though his dad wasn't a regular at his high school baseball games, sitting here watching the Wranglers play helped fill that void some. His dad may not have been a very good dad and he had always hated him for it but the effort his dad made now was enough. No matter how long they had.

His eyes made their way back to the small painting framed to the left of the room door. He hoped that the girl he saw walking through the sunflower field would let him in. He loved showing Melissa the physical therapy unit at the V.A. yesterday. Her eyes were bright and like always her concern for others was apparent. She invested in those around her even if it meant she gave up things for herself in doing so. He wanted to be a friend to her. The kind she seemed to be missing.

She appeared to have been really moved by her time with him yesterday. She had reached out to him. When he kissed her fingers, he could see that it had the same effect on her that it did on him. He could feel the goose bumps on her arm. He had missed getting to show her how much he cared with small acts of affection. When he looked at her lips and she didn't turn away, at first, he thought she wanted to kiss him as bad as he did her. Then she said she didn't think it'd be worth it. Had she not been loved like that lately? What about Wyatt's father? What if she was still involved with him? It'd been a week since he saw Wyatt at the baseball game. He still had so many questions and Melissa making him wait was starting to frustrate him. After they finished this article, he wasn't going to let her hold back anymore. He had to know.

******

On the way back to cancer center after lunch, Blake felt a little anxious. He was nervous for Melissa to sit with his dad. There were things she didn't know about their relationship. Blake had kept them from her when they were kids because he wanted to protect her. With his dad's change of heart, Blake hoped there wouldn't be anything said regarding Melissa. He hopped out of the truck and crossed the drop off lane. Melissa was sitting on a bench outside the cancer center.

Blake smiled. "Good morning! You're here early."

Her hair was pulled into a side ponytail with light curls falling over her shoulder. Her dark capris hit in the center of her calves curving down to the black sandals wrapped around her feet. The breeze caught some of the loose strands of hair around her face.

Blake swallowed. *Gosh, she's beautiful. I hope she knows it.*

She looked up and put her papers back in her purse. "Yeah. I'm trying to get my notes together so I can turn this article in by tomorrow." She stood and slipped her purse over her shoulder. "Are we ready to go in?"

Blake had debated if he should prepare Melissa or not about his dad's physical state. After seeing him this morning, Blake knew he had to. "There's something I need to prepare you for."

She paused, tilted her head slightly and pushed the loose strands from her eyes. "Ok."

He took a deep breath. "I got here early so I could see how dad was doing today. He's really just staying here because he doesn't have much time left. Possibly just a few months at best." He could see the sadness in her eyes. "He has really good days and he understands what you're saying to him but his physical appearance has decreased significantly since I have been here."

She nodded and said, "I understand."

"I just wanted you to be prepared that it may be worse than you expect." She didn't say anything but held his eyes. Blake sighed, "Ok, let's go in."

Melissa stayed close to him the whole way until they arrived outside his dad's door. As he reached for the door knob, she grabbed his opposite arm. He turned to look at her.

"Blake. I hope you know we didn't have to do this. I wouldn't want me meeting your dad to be a problem."

"I talked to him about it this morning. He said he would love it." He glanced down at her hand on his arm. She pulled it away back to her purse and nodded. Blake was sad at the loss of her touch. Blake pushed the door open and she again followed close behind him.

The room was in its usual darkened sterile state. Mr. Knoll was lying in bed with the sheets tucked tight around him and eyes closed. Blake walked over to his usual spot and leaned toward his dad's ear. "Dad, it's Blake."

Mr. Knoll slowly lifted his heavy eye lids. "Blake."

"Melissa is here for the interview if you're ready."

Mr. Knoll's smile spread across his face. "Of course. Can you help me sit up really good?" Blake hooked his arms under his dad's and helped slide him up straight in the bed. "Thanks, son. That's good."

Blake stepped back and turned to Melissa standing at the foot of the bed. "You can take this seat here next to dad and I will sit behind you." He flipped on the lamp behind her chair.

She smiled and nodded at him. Taking her seat next to the bed, she pulled out her notebook and started to get herself organized.

"Hello, Melissa." Mr. Knoll's raspy voice made her look up.

She smiled back at his sunken face. "Good afternoon, Mr. Knoll." She cleared her throat and said, "It's been a really long time."

He slightly shook his head in agreement. "It has. Melissa, I want to apologize to you for everything I said to you or about you. I was messed up."

Her eyebrows rose in surprise and she looked back at Blake. He nodded to her and only hoped his dad wouldn't go any further. Turning her head back to his dad she said, "Thank you."

Blake shot a sharp look at his dad who switched the conversation. "Thank you for doing the interview on Blake."

Melissa's face lit up with her bright smile. "Of course. Our service men deserve to be honored."

Blake was relieved his dad had stayed true to his word about Melissa. He stood at the end of the bed gripping the rail as he studied them. Their conversation was light and respectful. He knew it would be a big surprise to Melissa. He was sure all she remembered was a drunk yelling unhappy man.

As they continued to talk he felt his shoulders relax. He turned and took a seat under the TV. The air that Melissa had around her was contagious. She was sympathetic, always had been. Her heart was pure and honest, except when it came to him. Blake bit his cheek in an effort to keep his frustration at bay. He still couldn't understand why she wouldn't explained the past. There was still a gap between them. He just wanted to know and move past it.

Once again his own heart felt crushed by the weight of what the last 8 years must have been like for her. If she was the same Melissa, which he had a hunch she was, he knew that she was probably neglecting herself. Her dark brown eyes, though bright toward others, had moments of heaviness far behind them. She tried so hard to hide them, but it was there. He could see it. In the past he would've done everything he could to take that away regardless of her cute protest. *Man, she was stubborn.* He smiled to himself.

"So what do you think about your son being in the Marines? A Marine Raider at that?" Melissa's voice was smooth and upbeat.

"I am very proud of Blake. For him to come from a broken home and pretty much nonexistent father, he has become quite a remarkable young man. I wasn't the father I should've been to him but somehow he hasn't let the past hold him back." Mr. Knoll looked past Melissa through the window. "He is strong in character and confident in his convictions. Most of all he is here with me now. Even when I know I don't deserve his kindness, he's here."

Blake swallowed hard at hearing the words come out of his dad's mouth. They hadn't really talked about it even though Blake knew his dad was trying to show his appreciation. Melissa looked over toward him and he noticed her eyes were teary. He had to pull his gaze away from her or he would lose the tight grip he was straining to keep on his own damp eyes.

They continued talking about Blake as a young boy and what he was doing now at the V.A. hospital. Mr. Knoll sounded proud which caused a pull in Blake's chest. He'd always wanted to make his dad proud, but never seemed to accomplish it. As he sat in silence watching them, he realized that his heart was softening. Both of the people sitting across the room from him were dear to him. They meant more to him than he let himself realize until that very moment.

Knock Knock.

Blake jumped at the sound.

"Mr. Knoll, it's Doctor Jackson." The man was wearing a long white jacket and his hair was a pepper grey but his face was warm. "Oh, you have visitors." He extended a hand, "Hello, Blake."

Blake took his hand. "Good afternoon." He turned and held out his hand in direction of Melissa. "This is Melissa Adair. Melissa this is dad's doctor."

"Doctor Jackson, it's nice to meet you." Melissa said shaking his hand. She picked up her things and joined Blake at the end of the bed. "Should I wait outside?" she whispered.

"No it's ok. I want you to stay."

Dr. Jackson held out a chart Blake hadn't noticed at first. "How are you today, Mr. Knoll?"

"Good. Enjoying the company."

Dr. Jackson checked all the machines and wrote down his findings. "Good." He looked toward Blake and Melissa. "I'm glad you're here because I got the test results back."

Blake could instantly tell it wasn't good. The doctor paused for a moment. "It's spreading rather quickly. We've been doing light chemo per your request and it is no longer effective. We can always increase treatment if you wish. But I'm afraid it won't do much good."

Mr. Knoll leaned his head back and took a deep breath staring at the ceiling. Blake had known this day was coming but honestly thought that it wouldn't be this soon. It was as if the air was sucked from his lungs and he was suffocating. He couldn't do anything about this, no one could. Blake suddenly felt the warmth of Melissa's hand wrapping around his. He kept his eyes on his dad waiting for his response.

"I'm not sure that it's a decision I can make right now."

Dr. Jackson put his hand on Mr. Knoll's shoulder. "I understand. We will continue with no change in treatment until you let me know." And with that the doctor excused himself.

Blake couldn't make himself move. He just watched his dad lying motionless and then shift his eyes out the window. Melissa leaned into him and said, "I think I am going to go." She took a step forward to the end of the bed. "Mr. Knoll, thank you for visiting with me."

Mr. Knoll refocused back on her. "It was a pleasure, Melissa."

She stepped back and looked at Blake. He took her hand and said, "Let me walk you out."

He quietly led her out into the hallway not releasing her hand. He continued down toward the common area and vending machines. He could've held onto her hand forever, but he reluctantly released it. "Thanks for coming and visiting with him. I'm sorry it didn't last very long. But I could tell he enjoyed it."

"He's not the only one." She offered him a weak smile as she fidgeted with her purse strap. Without thinking he took her in his arms. He would've liked to say that it was for her comfort but it was really for his own. She slowly wrapped her arms around his waist and hugged him back. Blake's spirits rose as he closed his eyes trying to memorize the feel of her melting into him. There is no telling how long they stood there simply comforting each other. She began to loosen her grip and though he hated to, Blake let go.

"Thank you for coming, but not just for the interview." He slid his hands into his pockets.

She smiled back up to him. "Of course."

They stood in silence for a moment. "Did you give any thought to my offer for this weekend?" Blake asked.

"Actually I did. If you're still ok with it, I think Wyatt and I *will* join you." She smiled that beautiful smile.

"Great!" That didn't even begin to explain how he felt. "Do you guys want to just meet me outside of the stadium?" He couldn't help but sound excited.

She chuckled a little. "Yeah. I have your number so I'll let you know when we get there. Wyatt will be so excited."

"I'm glad." Without thinking he pulled her into another hug. Again Melissa melted into him. They held each other for a moment until she leaned back to look at his face. He got the sudden urge to kiss her, but stopped himself after what happened yesterday. Instead, Melissa pushed up on her toes and kissed his cheek, lingering a few seconds.

"I'll see you tomorrow. Bye, Blake." She turned to head to the elevator.

Blake watched her make her way around the corner. It took everything he had not to turn his head and with her lips on his check. He leaned against the wall and let his head fall back against it.

Oh, Melissa.

She had been so gracious in how she was handling the interview. He loved the way she was with the veterans at physical therapy. She laughed and smiled as she interacted with the patients. Her shoulders were relaxed and movements smooth. She wasn't guarded at all and it was beautiful. And now she was tender and compassionate to a man that in the past she didn't have much respect for, a man that was part of the reason Blake couldn't find Melissa. The tension in her back had eased and she had leaned forward to listen to Mr. Knoll speak. If only she'd do that with him.

Chapter 15

Melissa rubbed her thumb around the joint of her mug handle. Her mind had been on Mr. Knoll since she left the hospital two days ago. She knew it was going to be difficult to be in the cancer center, but she didn't expect to be present for such a personal meeting with the doctor. Blake was more shaken up than he probably meant to let on. This time it wasn't because of what Mr. Knoll had done but rather what was happening to him. She didn't know what to expect in seeing Blake today. Perhaps he needed a break at the game as bad as she needed a break from her tutoring papers.

Wyatt ate his ham and cheese sandwich and chips. He had on his Wranglers t-shirt and baseball hat. He was so excited and Melissa just loved watching him try to be patient and finish his lunch. He took his plate to the sink and then retrieved another water bottle from the fridge. She cleaned the counter and headed to her bedroom.

Looking in the mirror she couldn't help but analyze herself. She pulled her loosely curled hair into a ponytail and slipped through the hole in the back of her Wranglers baseball hat. The wisps of hair that never stayed back fell to the sides of her face. Her eyes dropped to her simple t-shirt and favorite blue jeans. At least she was going to be comfortable. She turned and headed to the living room. She checked her wallet for the cash she got out of the ATM earlier. She stopped at the front door. "Wyatt, are you ready to go?"

"Yeah, let's go!" He bolted to the door and she held it open for him.

As they made their drive to the stadium, she couldn't help but notice her pulse was beginning to pick up. Blake was an old friend who had offered to make up for them not going to the aquarium. An old friend that she used to be head over heels for. An old friend that almost kissed her. An old friend that she wanted to kiss back. An old friend she'd wanted a future with. An old friend she still had feelings for. She blew out a slow breath trying to calm her nerves.

She parked the car and pulled her phone out to text Blake and let him know they were there. She and Wyatt hopped out of the car and headed through the parking lot. She kept her eyes peeled for Blake at the entrance. She spotted him standing by the curb. Their eyes met and he gave her that all too perfect crooked smile and waved. She felt her knees give just a little. He was so handsome. She had done her best to help Wyatt know that Blake was an old friend who had some extra tickets. She didn't know what else to say because she didn't introduce him to guys often, if ever.

They joined Blake and she couldn't help but smile back. Looking at Wyatt she introduced them. "Wyatt, this is an old friend of mine, Blake Knoll."

"Didn't you come to one of my games?" Wyatt was clearly trying to place Blake.

"I did. I'm friends with Coach James too."

"Awesome! Hey, thanks for letting us come with you." Wyatt looked up at Blake and extended his hand.

Blake smiled and shook it. "Nice to meet you again, Wyatt. You can call me Blake." He looked into Melissa's eyes and her pulse raced again. It should be a sin to look so good. "Let's head inside."

They followed Blake to the gate and he presented their tickets. They got drinks and then found their seats. She let Wyatt sit first and then took her seat next to him. She slid her purse under her seat and placed her drink in the cup holder. The chair arm flexed and she was intensely aware that Blake was sitting down next to her. She leaned back in her seat and looked out at the field careful not to touch Blake's arm.

"He's really excited, isn't he?" Blake said leaning forward to look at Wyatt who was looking at the program.

She followed Blake's eyes and smiled. "He is." She looked back at Blake. "Thank you for this. I've only been able to bring him one time this year. We don't get to come as much as I'd like."

"Of course. Thanks for coming with me." He leaned back in his seat and took a drink. His arm settled on the arm rest next to her and she felt his bicep brush hers. Butterflies took off in her stomach.

After leaving the cancer center, Melissa had thought all night about Blake. She could see the change in Mr. Knoll and it had surprised her. She was thrown off by his apology to her. He appeared to really have had a change of heart. Blake hadn't pushed her away when the doctor came in. He kept her close, which was more than she could say about herself. When he held her in a tight embrace, she wanted to kiss him so badly, but at the last second she kissed his check. She wished she could jump blindly without fear of being hurt. Blake hadn't held back trying to get her to open up. She knew it was her turn.

"How did the article go when you turned it in yesterday?" Blake asked.

"I feel really good about it." She took a sip from her straw. "I can't believe the 4th of July is next week. This summer is just flying by."

"I understand. Before you know it, James and Cami's wedding will be here."

His mention of their wedding reminded Melissa that Blake was going to be a part of it. "Yeah. Cami is so excited but panicking as well." They shared an understanding light chuckle. It was true that Cami hadn't changed much since high school. Cami was flighty and high maintenance. Everything was exaggerated and dramatic. She and Blake used to joke about it a lot.

Wyatt cheered as the game began. He pointed out all the different stats about the game and players. He had something to say about each player at bat, mainly critiquing their swings. It was easy for Wyatt to talk to Blake and ask his opinion regarding the game.

Blake was so sweet to answer the ones that he knew. Melissa was really enjoying herself. Blake was the same gentleman he had always been and she was grateful. He wasn't pushing himself on her or Wyatt, which she could only pray would help limit Wyatt's questions about him later. She wasn't sure what her answer would be.

She couldn't help but feel bad that Wyatt didn't have a father figure to talk about stats and go to games with. Listening to them made her wonder what it would be like if Blake could be that for Wyatt. He would be a great dad, possibly because he knew everything he didn't want to be as a result of his own childhood. She had dreamed of them having children together and he had been excited every time they talked about it. She squeezed her eyes shut at the memory.

"Are you doing ok?" Blake asked.

"Yeah. Why?" Melissa looked up at him surprised that he had been watching her.

"You just looked a little lost there."

"Oh, I'm just enjoying the time with Wyatt. I wish I could do things like this more often." She looked back out at the field. "It's something that I struggle with."

"What do you mean?" He hadn't taken his eyes off her.

"Being a single mom is… I don't know." She paused to find the words. "I have to be both mom and dad to him. I guess I wonder if I'm being the best parent for him since I can't give him everything I want to."

******

Blake reached for her hand before he thought about it. "Melissa." She looked up at him. "Don't ever think that. I see Wyatt's eyes when he looks at you. His eyes shine when he talks to you and he listens to what you have to say. He appreciates you. I hope you can see it too."

He rubbed his thumb over the top of her hand. She took a deep breath and looked down at their hands. Blake followed her eyes down and slowly let go. He rubbed his hands on his lap trying to calm the warm tingling sensation moving from the tips of his fingers to his shoulders. He checked his peripheral vision to see if she was having the same problem as he was. Her long brunette hair was pouring out of the back of her baseball cap and brushed the back of her neck. The small strands graced her cheek bones and moved with the breeze across her face. Her eyes were shaded by the bill of her cap but he could still see the swirl of green in her brown eyes.

The rest of the game Blake just observed Melissa with Wyatt. She was a great mother and he wished there was some way that he could show her that. He had heard the brokenness in her voice when she talked about it earlier. She was doing an amazing job and it was evident that Wyatt loved her. They laughed together and it warmed Blake's heart that they had a good relationship. He was a little jealous of that.

"Before everyone starts to leave I'm going to take him to the bathroom." Melissa said leaning into him.

As she started to push off the arm rest to stand, he placed his hand on top of hers. "Let me take him." Seeing the hesitation in her eyes, he continued, "It's ok. I don't mind."

She relaxed her shoulders and settled back into her seat. "Let me ask him if that's ok." She turned to Wyatt. "Wyatt, Blake is going to take a quick bathroom break. Do you want to go with him before we get on the road?"

Wyatt leaned forward before standing. "I guess."

Blake stepped out and allowed Wyatt to lead the way up the steps.

"Hey, bud, are you having a good time?" Blake asked.

Wyatt jumped a little as he walked. "Yes! I love the Wranglers! I want to be one when I grow up."

"A baseball player?" Blake asked.

"Yep! James says if I practice real hard I can do anything."

Blake smiled down at him. "That's exactly right. Keep up the hard work."

As they walked out of the bathroom, Blake looked down at Wyatt. "Let's go find your mom"

"Ok. Thanks for bringing us." Wyatt looked up at him and Blake could tell he wanted to say something else.

"What's on your mind?" Blake could tell Wyatt looked hesitant to say anything. "It's ok. You can tell me whatever it is."

"Mom's busy all the time and I know she needs more breaks. We don't do much."

Blake's heart sank. "She works hard to take care of you."

Wyatt nodded. "I know. But she's lonely."

"How do you know?" Blake figured as much, but hated that her son could tell too.

"She needs someone to take care of her like she does me."

"What about your dad?" Blake wasn't sure that was the best question to ask before talking to Melissa, but it came out before he could think about that.

Wyatt shrugged. "I don't know who my dad is. I've never met him."

This surprised Blake and he hadn't expected that at all. What was Melissa's relationship to Wyatt's father if Wyatt didn't know him?

"Please, don't tell her I said anything." Wyatt seemed worried about it.

Blake hated the thought of keeping something from Melissa, especially when it was about Wyatt. But he wanted Wyatt to feel safe in expressing his feelings. Blake smiled down at Wyatt. "I won't. Let's just keep this conversation between us." Wyatt nodded.

Melissa was waiting for them at the top of the stairs of their section. She smiled when she saw them approaching.

"Let's get out of here before people start making a break for it." She turned to Blake. "Thank you for taking him."

"No problem."

As they walked toward the exit Blake watched Wyatt and Melissa talk some more about the game and what he wanted to work on at their next practice. Blake couldn't get what Wyatt had said out of his mind.

Blake noticed Melissa was watching him. "What?"

Her head slightly tilted letting some light reach the upper half of her face. "Are you ok?" Her voice seemed sincere.

"Yeah, why do you ask?"

She studied his eyes. "You just seem a little… distant."

Blake straightened his shoulders. He probably did seem quiet. He was doing a lot of thinking. Earlier during the game, she had opened up about personal things with Wyatt and he tried to reassure her that she was doing a great job. It wasn't what he wanted her to share but at least it was something. Then listening to Wyatt talk about it even more had made Blake want to be the one to take care of Melissa. He wanted to be the one Wyatt had described. Then he remembered all his unanswered questions and he was suddenly pulled into a sea of doubt. So many unknowns and things he couldn't control. He felt the emotion build in his chest once again. Even with the doubt, he didn't want her to feel like he was closing off from her, ever.

"I never mean to be distant from you, Melissa. I'm here, always."

Her eyes searched his face as if she wasn't sure. Finally, she said, "I believe you."

"Do you?" he asked before he thought about it.

She licked her lips and pressed them together. "Yes."

"I can't help but think you *don't* believe I'll always be here for you." He felt his frustration building again because he desperately needed answers. "I'm the one who tried to come back because I loved you. And I'm here now even when—"

She leaned closer to his face and spoke low. "Blake, we'll have this talk but I can't do this right now." She dropped her eyes to Wyatt. "Let's get out of here before they lock us in."

Blake watched her and Wyatt walk through the gates. He didn't want her to ever feel like he wasn't there for her. It was something he had promised her a long time ago. *She* was the one who left him.

At his truck, he dropped his head and let out a frustrated sigh. He was in deep trouble. He was angry with her and worried that she would never open up, never be fully honest. But he knew that he longed for her, possibly more than he ever had before.

Chapter 16

As she combed through her hair, Melissa's mind couldn't help but think about the day ahead. Her article about Blake had run this week in the Shaw Creek Press. There had been a lot of praise for the article and it helped give her confidence in what she had written. She figured that Blake would've read it by now and she was nervous to see him at the recognition ceremony this afternoon. It had been a busy week and she had spent most of her time at the library. She was there every day doing research for her next article over the history of the town square. When they weren't at the library, Melissa took Wyatt to the park, practiced baseball in the back yard, or played games in the house.

After the way they left the Wranglers game a week ago, she hadn't heard one thing from Blake. Although she hadn't tried to contact him either. He must've been spending a lot of time away from his house because he didn't come home until after she went to bed most nights. She was worried that he was really mad at her and avoiding her. Which she knew she deserved. It had been two weeks since he told her he'd wait for her to tell him about what happened. The fear seemed to be holding her captive and she wasn't sure she was ready to face him. But with how frustrated he seemed, she was afraid she was losing her chance.

She checked her makeup one last time before straightening her patriotic blouse and adjusting the belt on her blue jeans. Once she felt satisfied she went down stairs and into the kitchen. Gram was wiping down the counters and her mom was putting the last dishes into the dish washer while Wyatt sat at the table eating a sandwich. "Is everyone about ready to leave?" she asked.

Gram's khaki pants paired well with her blue collard shirt and red lipstick. She smiled as she met Melissa. "Oh, yes. We're just cleaning up a little bit. I've been looking forward to this for a while now."

"You look beautiful, Mel." Julie leaned and kissed her cheek.

"Thanks, Mom."

"Let's go!" Julie turned and helped guide Gram out the front door slipping her purse over her shoulder.

Melissa slipped her small wallet into her pocket not wanting to lug a purse around the festival. Everyone made their way to her mom's SUV. She paused for Wyatt to get seated before getting in herself. Her eyes found their way to Blake's empty driveway. He must already be there. She slid in the seat next to Wyatt and buckled in. After several minutes of light conversation with Wyatt, Gram turned toward Melissa. "You did good, sweetie."

"What do you mean?" Melissa asked.

"The article. You did a great job on it." Gram's voice tender and soft.

"Thanks, Gram. I hope he thinks so."

"I'm sure he does. Blake is a good guy and you captured him beautifully with your words."

"Have you spoken to him?" Julie looked at her through the rearview mirror.

"Not since we saw him at the baseball game." She looked over at Wyatt who was looking out the window silent. They talked only briefly on the way home from the Wranglers game about Blake. She didn't want him to get attached to someone that might be moving back to North Carolina or end up not wanting anything to do with her. She may not be able to protect herself from disappointment, but she would try her hardest to protect Wyatt.

They continued their drive with Wyatt talking about all the things he wanted to do when they got there. Once parked, they weaved their way through the parking lot toward the tents and booths.

"I'm ready for some rides!" Wyatt pointed toward the ferris wheel at the far side of the park.

"In a little bit. We might even get Gram to ride that one." She winked at him. Melissa spotted Jade talking to Cami by one of the craft booths and they made their way toward them. "Hey, guys."

Jade gave her a big hug, "You look great, Mel."

"Thanks," she returned her smile.

"Hey!" Cami gave Gram a side hug. "I'm so glad you came with them. Someone's got to keep these kids in line."

"Hey, I'm not a kid," Julie said.

"You're my kid," Gram said and then winked at Cami. "I can almost hear the wedding bells ringing for you, Cami."

Her eyes lit up as she spoke. "I know! It's hard to believe it's less than one week away." She shot a look toward James. "I'm so excited about it!"

"You have no idea how much." James left a peck on Cami's cheek. James turned to Wyatt. "Hey, buddy. Do you want to go check out some of the games with me?"

"Sure! Can I, Mom?" Wyatt could hardly contain himself.

"Yes. Have fun. The ceremony is going to start shortly so listen for the announcement." Melissa watched them run off with Gram and Julie following close behind.

Jade locked arms with Melissa and they walked with Cami in the direction of the band stage. Then Melissa received an alert on her phone and she checked it.

"Who is it?" Cami asked.

"It's just one of the fellow teachers at the tutoring program." Melissa dropped her phone to her side as they continued to walk.

"Darn, I was hoping it was one of the guys I gave your number to last week," Cami teased.

"What?! You give my number out to strangers?" Melissa stopped in her tracks.

"They're not total strangers."

"Cami, you can't be serious!" Melissa stared at her. "I'm not going to go out with random guys you find."

Cami put a hand on her hip. "Why not? How else are you going to meet guys?"

"They're not Blake," Jade interrupted.

Melissa shot a quick look at her. "What's that supposed to mean?"

Cami laughed. "I have to agree with Jade."

Jade squeezed her arm. "Oh nothing."

Melissa rolled her eyes and kept walking. They continued to make their way through the lines of booths and Cami changed the subject to her wedding. The three of them rounded the corner and in the distance the stage came into view. Melissa spotted Blake standing next to the stairs talking with the mayor. He was wearing a short sleeve black pearl snap shirt that clung to his arms and chest. His deep blue jeans fit perfectly and settled around his black cowboy boots. Melissa sighed to herself. Why did he have to look so good?

"I'm going to go find James and everyone then meet you after the ceremony." Cami headed off in search of their family.

Their pace slowed to a crawl. Jade's eyes found the dirt path in front of them. "I read your article."

Hesitant, Melissa asked, "What did you think?" Her eyes dropped to the ground as well.

"I think it was very honorable of Blake and his service." Jade paused and then stopped walking. She looked up at Melissa. "Can I ask you something?"

"Yes," Melissa said slightly nervous.

"Are you having feelings for him again?" Jade's voice was sincere.

It was the one question she hadn't been able to get out of her mind but yet was too scared to answer. "Why do you ask?"

"Come on, Melissa. The way you wrote about him and you spent some personal time with him off the record. Not to mention the look on your face just now when you saw him."

Knowing she had been caught, Melissa looked toward the stage and struggled to answer. She knew she was torn between her fear and her heart.

Jade continued, "It's ok. You can be honest with me."

Looking back at Jade, Melissa answered, "I don't know. I mean, I'm afraid of how I feel. Plus, he's still waiting for a job offer in North Carolina. It's hard to admit I'm falling for him when he may not want me after he knows everything. I don't know that I deserve it."

Melissa felt Jade's squeeze from their still linked arms. "You deserve happiness, especially after what you went through. It was hell and I can say that because I was there. Blake deserves happiness too. The simple fact that he hasn't closed off from you after finding out about Wyatt should stand for something, right?"

"I guess." Melissa had to agree that Blake had been very accepting of Wyatt and the way he interacted with him at the game had melted her heart. "I'm not so sure it will stay that way."

"Blake isn't a horrible person, Mel. I know you aren't meant to live the rest of your life alone. Don't be afraid to fall for him again." She smiled and then began to lead Melissa forward. "I'll let it go for now. It's time to get ready for your presentation."

Melissa and Jade made their way to the stage where a small-town band was playing a cover of a well-known country song. There was a crowd that had formed with blankets and lawn chairs to enjoy the music. A mom was laughing at her baby while helping him bounce across their blanket. Near the food vendors, tables were filled with families eating their lunch. A little boy tried to take a huge bite of turkey leg as he followed his dad. Shaw Creek was a great place to live. One of the beautiful things about living in a small town was the ability to come together and celebrate the community.

Mrs. Hall was standing at the end of the stage fumbling through papers in her hands. She waved at them as they approach. "Melissa! We're ready to do the 'Hometown Hero' presentation. Here's the plaque for Blake Knoll." She handed it to Melissa. Melissa ran her fingers over Blake's engraved name. As the band finished their song, Mrs. Hall joined them on stage and took the microphone from their lead singer.

"Great job guys! How is everyone doing today?" The crowd cheered loudly. "I'm Susan Hall, the editor of the Shaw Creek Press. We are so glad you were able to join us for the 4th of July festival today. This year we wanted to honor one of our very own who served in the armed forces. We chose one from the many submitted names." She motioned toward Melissa to join her on stage.

"Melissa Adair interviewed the soldier and her story was published earlier this week. She did a great job of honoring our very own hometown hero."

Melissa inhaled quickly, trying to maintain her strong smile in anticipation of seeing Blake. She saw Jade join her family toward the front of the crowd. Mrs. Hall was giving a brief overview of her article to introduce Blake. Melissa's pulse increased and she spotted him at the bottom of the stairs on the opposite side of the stage. Mrs. Hall's voice became audible again.

"Please help me in welcoming our hometown hero to the stage, Blake Knoll."

The crowd stood and cheered as Blake stepped onto the stage. He smiled at Melissa before turning to the crowed and waved.

Mrs. Hall stood between Melissa and Blake. "Blake, we are so thankful for your service to our country. You have made your hometown very proud. We want to present you with this plaque in honor of service and sacrifice. Thank you."

Blake shook her hand and then stepped toward Melissa. She extended her hand. When the grooves of his hand pressed against her own, an indescribable shock made its way through her hand and up her arm. His blue eyes and white crooked smile had her locked in a trance. She forced her other arm to hand over the plaque. For a brief moment, his face was sincere and unguarded. Then he turned to face the crowd again.

How was Blake having such an intense effect on her? Melissa hadn't lied to Jade when she asked about her feelings toward Blake. She really didn't know what her heart felt, or wanted for that matter. That wasn't fair to Blake no matter how she tried to justify it to herself.

Chapter 17

Blake shook hands and enjoyed visiting with several of the people in the audience after the ceremony. He had appreciated the warm welcome and sentiments from everyone there. All his successes and failures during his time in the service were spent alone and now having people interested in his story made him happier than he could've thought. He was both honored and humbled.

On a side table, there were stacks of the Shaw Creek Press that featured Melissa's article about him. There were several people paying to pick one up. Blake figured they hadn't seen his story and wanted to read it now. He was really pleased with the article. Melissa still had a beautiful way of writing, even for an interview. He was touched by her words and he felt like they came from her heart and in return had stirred his.

Melissa.

It had been a week since he last saw her at the Wranglers game and he hadn't gotten a chance to tell her he appreciated the article yet. It crossed his mind to send her a text message or call to let her know he read the article, but he changed his mind. He had been mad, madder than he ever wanted to be at her. He didn't want to talk to her if she wasn't going to be open. So, he kept himself busy all week. He volunteered longer hours at the V.A. and immediately went to see his dad afterward. If his dad fell asleep early, he would go for a really long run down dirt roads on the other side of town. He needed to have a talk with her and he felt guilty that he'd done exactly what he was mad at her for doing. He closed himself off from her.

Blake turned to search the crowd for Melissa. He spotted her talking to her family and Jade across the lawn. He slowly approached them, not wanting to interrupt their conversation.

Jade saw him over Melissa's shoulder and greeted him. "Hi, Blake."

Melissa took a half step backward to allow Blake to enter their circle and gave him a half smile. He'd hoped to see her bright smile instead.

James stuck his hand out and shook Blake's hand. "Congrats, man. You're making a great impact. People are loving what you've been doing to help the wounded vets at the V.A."

Blake shrugged and said, "Well, you can't give me all the credit. Melissa did a great job on the article." He shot a quick look at her. She looked up at him and offered him a slightly brighter smile causing her eyes to crease some. With her loose curls gently brushed over her shoulders. *So beautiful.* He swallowed so not to say it out load in front of everyone for fear she'd be uncomfortable.

"Thank you, Blake. But it is your story. You're the hero." She held his gaze for a second and he wondered if she was feeling the pull just as much as him. She dropped her eyes and looked at Wyatt. "Are you wanting to check out some more games and rides?"

"Yes!" Wyatt smiled big at her.

Blake smiled to himself. He loved watching Melissa and Wyatt. They had a fun relationship, one he never had with his own mother.

"You know what I really want to do?" Melissa asked Wyatt.

"What?" Wyatt had to pause so not to run ahead of them.

Pointing she said, "I want to ride the ferris wheel."

Wyatt followed her pointing. "Ok!"

Melissa smiled and answered, "Ok, let's go." They turned to leave and then she paused. "Blake, why don't you join us for a while?"

He was elated that Melissa was inviting him along. "Are you sure? I don't want to impose."

Jade stepped next to Melissa and motioned for him to follow them. "Not at all! You're always welcome."

Melissa smiled at Jade then back at Blake and nodded.

Blake mostly stayed near James as they made their way through the festival. Even though James was talking to him, Blake couldn't take his eyes off Melissa most of the afternoon. She laughed and was relaxed with everything around her, except him. Wyatt brought out the best in her making her eyes bright and unguarded. As he watched her skipping around with Wyatt and goofing around, watching them playing the different toss games and riding the swings, Blake knew her life was full and it made him happy. He had originally thought perhaps she was struggling but he could now see how happy Wyatt made her. Blake felt a soft touch on his right arm and looked to see Gram.

"How are you, dear?" Her voice was warm like always and it was hard to not feel better when he was around her.

"I'm good, really good. How are you, Gram?"

She linked her arm in his and they slowly followed the others to the next booth. "I'm glad you stayed to spend the afternoon with us."

"Me too." More than he could say.

"I wanted to invite you to my birthday party tomorrow. It should be easy for you since you're just across the street." She smiled at him.

Knowing she wasn't going to take any excuse he smiled back. "I'd love to come."

They stood in silence watching James and Wyatt compete in the basketball toss. Blake couldn't help but laugh and cheer as they played. Every once in a while, Melissa would look at him but he had a hard time reading her eyes. At times, it was like she felt the same way he did and then other times, like she was fighting against it. He still needed to tell her how much the article meant to him.

"I'm really proud of you, Blake." He turned to see Gram's eyes full of acceptance and love. She looked toward Melissa and continued, "You've become a wonderful man. Some would agree with me but they just have a hard time showing it."

Blake followed Gram's eyes and he realized Gram was once again more perceptive in things than he thought. "I don't know, Gram. Time has changed us both... a lot."

She lightly nodded her head in agreement. "Yes, but you have so much love to give and you were willing to give it to her in the past." She paused as if deep in thought. "Regardless of the past, regardless of what has happened since, don't dismiss the chance of getting to love again."

Blake looked back at her. She could see that his feelings were stronger than he was trying to let on. It wasn't worth trying to hide them from Gram. "I don't know that she wants to love me again. I still don't know why she left me to begin with. I told her I'd wait until she was ready to tell me everything." He looked back at Melissa. "What if her reason is harder to take than I thought?"

Gram was silent. Blake figured she was debating on how much to share. After a while he asked one of the questions he feared to know the answer to. His voice almost a whisper. "And what if she doesn't want to love me again?"

Gram squeezed her hand against his forearm. "Trust me, Blake. She may be in denial about what her heart feels, but she wants to be loved. No matter what form that takes. God created us to love and puts that in our hearts. Especially when we think we've lost our ability to."

Her words were filled with wisdom and he knew they held value. Seeing himself loving Melissa wasn't the question. He'd always loved her, even after he finally decided to try and move on. The feelings that were rising inside of him were no longer something he wanted to push back. He respected Melissa and whatever her past held but it was risky. Allowing his heart to fall for her again but it was already too late to stop the fall.

They caught up with everyone at the next booth. "I think I'm ready to call it a day." Gram said, the exhaustion in her voice apparent.

Melissa came to her side. "We can go, Gram."

"James and I can take them home." Cami interjected. "You didn't get to ride the ferris wheel." Cami winked at her.

Melissa started to argue. "Don't be. I'm ready to go—"

"It's settled. Blake can bring you home since he lives across the street." Cami grabbed Wyatt's hand and headed toward the parking lot. James shrugged and smiled as Gram locked her arm around his elbow.

"I'm going to head home too," Jade leaned in and kissed Melissa's cheek. Blake wasn't sure if she said something to her or not but Jade sent him a wink as she walked away. Melissa turned around to face him and had a strained look on her face.

"What's wrong?" Blake asked.

"Nothing." She started fidgeting with the hem of her shirt.

He didn't want her to be uneasy when they were alone, quite the opposite actually.

"Hey, how about we try some of this amazing fried food and then head to the ferris wheel. I've not been on one in forever." He tried to lighten the mood so she would be comfortable with him again.

Her shoulders relaxed. "That sounds good. I'm pretty hungry."

After a quick debate, they each got a corndog. They slowly walked through the vendors eating their food as they headed to the rides. Now that they were alone, Blake could tell her about the article. "Thanks for the article. I've not had a chance to tell you. You still have a way with words."

She tucked her hair behind her ear exposing the curve in her neck and Blake had to look away so he wasn't tempted to make a move. *Not yet.*

"Thanks. I'm glad you liked it."

He could tell she was still needing a minute to relax with him. "It meant a lot and I can't thank you enough for doing it."

Melissa nodded and then slowed as they approached the ferris wheel line. She looked up and smiled, "I forgot how tall these things are."

"You did want to ride."

Melissa looked up at the spinning lights and smiled. "I do. Let's go."

They got in the short line waiting for the next car to come. Blake stood silently beside her. He could see how much she loved it as the lights bounced off her eyes. Melissa entered the car and slid to the far side. Blake slid in and sat next to her, letting his leg press firmly against hers. She turned looking out over her side as they began to move. The sunset was glowing on her skin and the look on her face was pleasant. She was happy. He loved seeing her like this, the way she was in the sunflower field. "You're the same you know?"

She turned her head to him. "What do you mean?"

"You laugh often, soak in the little things, and most of all you love deeply." He could see the pulse rise on her neck. He didn't move as if suspended like the car they were riding.

The ferris wheel came to a stop with them at the top. They still hadn't broken eye contact. He wanted her to know that he meant the things he said and more importantly that he wanted her to believe it.

"I'm not so sure I agree with all of that." Her voice soft.

Blake couldn't believe that she always saw the good in others and doubted she could do the same. She believed in the kids she taught, encouraging them to succeed. She supported Jade in her restaurant and bragged about her cooking. She breathed hope, confidence, and love into Wyatt. Blake wanted so bad to make her feel the worth she possessed.

Without thinking, he leaned toward her, closing the space between them. He cupped her face with one of his hands and felt the heat from her face infuse his fingers. She didn't flinch or pull away like he had expected. Forgetting all caution, he let his lips find hers. She was soft and sweet and it was better than he remembered. Everything inside him surged. It was an interlacing of the past, present, and future desires. It was a passion he had almost forgotten. He kissed her slow and longingly, pouring everything he had into it. Then he felt something he hadn't expected, causing him to release her lips and pull back.

Tears ran down her face and pooled on his thumb. Gently he wiped them from her face and dropped his hand. Fear overcame him and he hoped he hadn't made things worse. Struggling to find his breath he whispered, "I'm sorry."

She shook her head as she looked down at her lap. "No, it's ok."

The ferris wheel began moving again and he leaned back against the chair. She tilted her head back with eyes closed and Blake feared he had made a dreadful mistake. He only wanted her to know she could be loved and be loved by him. Was she crying because he had kissed her? Was it because she knew she wanted to kiss him back? So many questions swirled in his head that as the wheel moved again, he almost got dizzy. "Melissa?"

She didn't look at him but said, "It's ok."

They exited the car and started making their way away from the ride. He walked with his hands in his jeans and was scared to look over at her. Her body was ridged and pulled back. She was guarding herself.

They came up to the edge of the parking lot and slowed to a stop. Blake searched for the right words to say but Melissa spoke first.

"Thanks, Blake. It meant a lot what you said, even if I don't know that I agree with all of it." She offered him a weak smile.

"Thank you for all you did with the article. I can't tell you how amazing it was. You still write beautifully." He returned her smile. "Dad had a great time with you and it turned out amazing."

"I'm glad." She looked out toward the cars and then back to him. "Blake, I've been doing a lot of thinking this week. I know you were angry and I don't fault you for that at all. I'm angry at myself too."

"I'm sorry I let myself get that way, especially in front of Wyatt."

"I appreciate that." She pulled her bottom lip into her mouth. "I'm going to be busy with Cami's wedding coming up this week. She's wanting to spend three days in Dallas as part of her bachelorette party. Can we maybe talk after I get back?"

"We're alone now," he stated.

"Blake, I want to tell you everything and answer your questions. I do." She swiped a tear that escaped down her cheek. "I'm just really messed up and then we just kissed and I don't know…"

"I feel like you're making excuses."

Her face turned hot. "You know, Blake, you're right. I am. I've wanted to have this talk with you for years. Now that you're back I've cowered away every chance I get." She took a shaky breath. "You're making me feel things again, things I haven't felt in a really long time. I'm scared."

He took a step toward her. "Mel, I'm scared too. I've got a number of different scenarios running through my head I can't even tell them apart anymore. You're not the only one with feelings."

"I know that."

"I don't think you do. You're just worried about getting hurt yourself. What about me? What about me eight years ago? You cared that little for me?" He could hear himself getting louder with every question.

She straightened her back. "I did care about you back then. I've never stopped. I do now. I chose to push you away when I found out I was pregnant because I didn't want it to be a problem for YOU! I wanted you to have the happy life you didn't have as a kid. I may have been wrong, but at the time I thought it was the best thing for you."

Blake couldn't believe what she said. "You think leaving me alone was the best thing for me?!"

"I panicked, Blake." Tears ran down her face. "I panicked," she said again breathless. She wiped her face. The anguish was evident on her face and seeing some people looking at them as she said, "I'm going to go. There's more but I can't right now." With that she turned and disappeared between the cars.

Blake's heart fell to his feet. He knew he had taken a risk by spending alone time with her, let alone kissing her. How could she say she pushed him away and crushed his heart so that he could be happy? It had completely shattered his world.

He slowly walked out toward his truck and climbed inside. His plaque was sitting in the passenger's seat where he left it after the ceremony. Their time together doing the interview had been great. He'd allowed himself to see himself in her life again. He started the engine and then leaned his head against his headrest. Sure, he was given a great award, but it wasn't the one he really wanted. He wanted a beautiful brown-eyed girl, the only girl he'd ever loved. Now he wasn't so sure it would ever happen.

Chapter 18

Melissa pulled the cake out of the oven and placed it on the counter. The smell of chocolate filled the kitchen making her mouth water. While it cooled, she mixed the icing in a bowl.

"My my. Something smells wonderful in here." Gram entered the kitchen behind her.

"I hope so, Gram. It is *your* birthday." She pushed the icing down the sides of the cake. Gram grabbed a bowl and started mixing her pasta salad together. "Gram, don't do that. It's your birthday. You're not supposed to be in the kitchen."

Gram swatted Melissa's hand from her bowl and huffed. "What, you think that because I'm eighty I can't help with my birthday meal?"

Melissa knew better than to try to kick Gram out of her own kitchen. "Alright." She went back to icing the cake smiling to herself. "How many are you expecting, Gram?"

"Let's see." She looked out the kitchen window trying to recall everyone. "Julie, you, and Wyatt. Cami and James said they'd bring drinks. Your Aunt Sarah said she was bringing your cousins, Aly and Luke."

"Great! We'll have a good crowd. I haven't seen Aly and Luke in forever!" She licked her fingers as she put the empty icing bowl in the sink. Aly was a great cousin and an even better friend, like Jade. They all graduated the same year and stayed close throughout college. Aly was the outgoing crazy one. Jade was the logical call-it-like-it-was one. When they were together Melissa definitely had her hands full.

"Oh and Blake said he would come."

Melissa dropped the whisk in the glass bowl, making a load noise. "What?"

Gram didn't look up from her pasta salad but Melissa could see her sneaky smirk. "I invited him yesterday at the festival."

"Why would you do that?" Melissa asked.

Gram turned to her and put her hand on her hip. "It's my birthday and I wanted him to come. Why should it be a problem for you?"

Melissa shook her head then finished icing the cake. Pressing her palms to the cool counter top, she tried to push back the memory of last night. Just the two of them above the festival with the cool summer breeze gently rocking the ferris wheel car. The way his arm pressed against her own and feeling herself flush from the contact. The smell of his cologne infusing the air around them. The words he said, the look in his eyes, the touch of his hands, and the taste of his lips. Then the heat in his voice as he questioned her about talking to him. She felt the same panic in her chest that she had felt last night. Melissa squeezed her eyes shut shaking the memory and doing her best to return to the kitchen.

"It's not a problem if Blake comes. I just didn't expect you to invite him." Melissa turned to retrieve the burgers from the fridge letting the air cool her flushed face.

If he came to the party how would he act? The interview and time at the hospital with his dad had made Melissa let her walls down a little bit. Then they had a great time with Wyatt at the baseball game. It wasn't part of the interview but it felt comfortable and natural. The truth was she had missed Blake's friendship. The doubt she had about her own feelings were still there but she still questioned his feelings. What had that kiss meant? Was it because he felt sorry for her? They had loved each other once. Then when she told him why she pushed him away, well part of it, he got angry. She wasn't sure what to expect in seeing him after that.

She placed the patties on the counter and turned to see the kitchen was empty. Where did Gram go? Melissa moved to the doorway and saw Gram and Wyatt greeting the family at the front door.

"Melissa!" Aly rushed over and wrapped her arms around Melissa. "It's so good to see you. Wyatt is getting so big!"

Melissa stepped back and looked over at Wyatt giving Luke a high-five. "He really is."

"How have you been?" Aly's voice was happy and upbeat. She reminded Melissa of Cami. She was outgoing, never met a stranger, and of course beautiful.

They turned to head into the kitchen. "I'm doing really good. It's summer break so I've been busy with Wyatt playing baseball and then tutoring at the library. What about you?"

Aly took a seat at the kitchen island. "I'm doing good. The insurance office is good, but I'm worried things may be changing soon. Some things have happened and I'm not sure I'll be able to stay there much longer."

"I'm sorry to hear that, Al." Melissa grabbed two water bottles and joined her at the island. She could tell Aly was trying to hide how upset it made her.

Aly took the bottle and cleared her throat. "It's ok. I'm not sure what I want to do with my life anyway. It's funny how we've been out of college for so long and I still feel like I don't know what to do."

Melissa's heart ached for Aly. It wasn't easy not knowing what to do with your life. She'd been there before. "Maybe you need to take a break. Clear your head and then look at the things you like to do."

Aly nodded. "That's not a bad idea. You never know I might move in with Jade and do something here."

"That's a great idea." Melissa could tell there was more to the story but didn't want to push her. Aly was always private about personal things. She loved the idea of Aly moving closer. She'd missed having her close like Jade. Then the three of them could do more together again, like old times.

Luke busted through the doorway and shoved Aly off her seat. "Hey, Melissa! Blink twice if she hasn't stopped talking." Aly slapped his arm.

Laughing Melissa shook her head. "Oh, Luke. It's good to see you two haven't changed."

"Well, what can I say? I just love my baby sister." Luke looked around the island. "Gram asked me to get the burgers on the grill."

Melissa pointed and said, "Behind you."

"Thanks," Luke grabbed the platter and headed out the back door.

"You guys crack me up." Melissa said turning back to Aly.

They continued to get the other side dishes ready while everyone else visited in the living room. Once everything was prepped, Aly helped Melissa carry everything out to the back patio.

"Melissa, how are you?" Her Aunt Sarah came out with everyone and gave her a hug.

"I'm good," Melissa answered. Then handed Sarah a glass of sweet tea.

"Oh, thank you. Wyatt was so excited to tell me all about his games and that he got to go to a Wranglers game." Her aunt took a drink of her tea.

"Yeah. He loves baseball." Melissa started setting out the plates and napkins.

Luke flipped the burgers and called out, "I've got about three more minutes and burgers will be ready."

Gram stepped up next to Melissa and nudged her. "Someone's late."

Melissa nodded knowing there was no need trying to act like she didn't care. The only thing she had going for her was there was no way Gram knew how their night ended. Melissa was happy she hadn't pried about it either.

"You ought to go check on him. You know, tell him I won't take any of his excuses." Her teasing tone made Melissa smile. It was hard not to smile around Gram.

"Maybe he's busy, Gram." Melissa insisted.

"His truck is in the drive and I won't take no for an answer. It's my birthday." Gram patted Melissa's arm. "Thank you, dear."

Melissa sighed knowing she couldn't get out of it. She was going to walk over there and ask Blake to come to the party, for Gram. Melissa shook her head and turned to head across the street.

Blake's living room light was on and his old truck was backed in the driveway. Melissa slowly stepped up to his front door and took a deep breath. She rang the doorbell and straightened her shoulders. Blake greeted her with a smile and looked surprised to see her. "Melissa?"

She took a deep breath fighting the butterflies forming in her stomach. "Gram sent me over." He looked a little disappointed so she clarified. "She told me to tell you she wasn't taking any of your excuses."

He smiled that crooked smile and her resolve to stay calm began to shake. She laced her fingers in front of her and smiled back.

"I did say I was going to come, didn't I?" He looked at her with what seemed like longing. "I wasn't sure it was a good idea."

She smiled knowing that he must've been thinking about last night like she had. "Well, it's hard to say no to Gram. And I am pretty sure she would have my hide if I didn't bring you back with me."

He nodded and chuckled, releasing some of the tension around them. "Alright, let's go."

When they entered the back yard, Melissa figured she better make light of the situation so people didn't get the wrong idea. "Look who else Gram invited."

Blake settled into an easy conversation about his time in the service and the situation with his dad. Her family had always been an open door to him. Luke and Blake joked and talked baseball, it made her happy to hear him laugh. Wyatt convinced them to toss a baseball and Melissa settled in next to Aly on the outdoor furniture.

"He sure is handsome," Aly said following Melissa's eyes out to the yard. "I bet the dress blues look better than that old high school baseball uniform."

Melissa rolled her eyes. "Aly, please."

"So what's the story with you two?"

Melissa clasped her hands in her lap. "Nothing."

"Come on, Melissa. I see you watching him. Not to mention the look in his eyes when he looks at you." Aly looked back at the boys in silence for a few beats. "It wouldn't be a bad thing for it to be more than nothing."

Melissa tried to sound as indifferent as she could. "I don't know about that."

"Don't shut out the idea." She laid her head on Melissa's shoulder. "He might just surprise you."

Melissa watched Blake laughing with Luke and her mind questioned what Aly just said. Would Blake surprise her? The last time she didn't think so and she had broken both of their hearts. "He told me to wait until I was ready to tell him everything."

"I think that's awfully noble of him. If it were me I'd be demanding answers. Plus, he seems ok about Wyatt."

"He kissed me last night after everyone left. Then we got in an argument about me hiding things from him and how he wanted me to just tell him."

Aly sighed. "What did you tell him?"

"I got mad and defensive. I told him I chose to push him away because I wanted him to be happy. He didn't believe me. I left before telling him about..." Her voice trailed off. It still wasn't easy talking about it. Melissa watched as Wyatt high-fived Blake and Luke after hitting the ball high in the air to them. Her heart clenched a little. "He's still waiting to hear about a possible job in North Carolina. What if I tell him everything and trust that we can move forward only to have him leave?"

Aly slid her arm around Melissa's elbow and held her tight. "You have to decide if it's worth the risk?"

"And if it is?" Melissa asked.

Aly sighed dropping her shoulders. "Then you have to be willing to wait. That's the real question. Will you trust that he will stay with you and wait for him this time? He may need some time after finding out. Will you give him the chance to come back?"

Melissa couldn't admit to Aly that things were more than just nothing. She was positive Aly already knew, along with everyone else. Falling for Blake was something she found herself struggling to keep from doing. But her fear of rejection still held her heart captive. Yes, she hadn't waited for him to return. She didn't give him the chance to stay before, but there was no guarantee he would choose to stay now. She knew she wasn't giving him much of a reason to stay either. The answer to Aly's question still lingered in the back of her mind. Was the possible pain and sting of rejection worth the risk? Melissa knew she couldn't answer it yet.

Chapter 19

Blake walked down the long hospital hallway feeling better than he had since his fight with Melissa at the festival. Spending the afternoon with Melissa's family had been good for him. Everyone had greeted him warmly offering hugs. They treated him just like everyone else there. They had an open seat for him at their table and they included him in every conversation. It was a sense of real family, something he had missed. Even Melissa had been nice. They didn't talk much other than in group conversation but he was glad they'd been ok around each other.

He retrieved his water bottle from the vending machine and made his walk toward his dad's room. Before getting to the door, Dr. Jackson stopped him in the hall.

"Blake, I wanted to talk to you before you see your dad."

Blake could tell it wasn't going to be good. "Ok."

Dr. Jackson released a sigh then spoke. "It's been over a week now since our conversation about stopping treatment for your dad. I know that it's a hard subject to talk about but I don't see the point of continuing treatment. He gets weak and sleeps most of the day, especially when he has chemo. When he doesn't have chemo, he seems to be in a daze. He is barley eating and has to be assisted with drinking now." He paused. "Can you visit with him today about his options?"

Blake nodded his head in understanding. "How long does he really have?"

Dr. Jackson said, "It's hard to say. The past month he has declined quickly. Some days I think he could have a while but if I'm realistic, he probably has four weeks at best."

The statement hit Blake's chest like the butt of a machine gun. He knew his dad seemed worse but to only have a month? He shook the doctors hand and turned toward the door. He dropped his head and almost couldn't bring himself to open it. Blake never dreamed he'd be having this conversation with his dad. He took a deep breath and opened the door.

The room looked the same as it did every day when Blake came to visit. The sun light from the window seemed darker than normal. Perhaps some clouds were rolling in. His dad lay still with eyes closed, only the beeps of machines and slow rise and fall of his chest were proof of life. Trying hard not to disturb anything, Blake took his seat next to the bed. This time instead of waking him he just sat and stared at the white floor. The mangled mess of emotions running through Blake were a mixture of everything he'd felt and battled his whole life. The anger, disappointment, resentment, peace, safety, purpose, loneliness, comfort, and love all fought for the primary place in his heart.

Suddenly there was movement in the bed. Mr. Knoll turned and smiled. "Blake, can you hand me another blanket?" His voice was a groggy whisper.

"Sure, Dad." Blake got up and went to the closet to grab another blanket. He walked back over and draped it over his dad. He couldn't help but notice that his dad's fingers were nothing but bone and they couldn't even grip enough to pull the blanket up to his chin. His face was pale and sunken. Blake took the edge of the sheet and pulled it up for him. Then Blake took his seat next to his dad and turned to look out the window. The pending conversation was almost more than Blake could stand. If he was honest, Blake wasn't sure he was ready to accept the inevitable.

"Ah, much better," Mr. Knoll dropped his shoulders trying to relax. They sat quietly until Mr. Knoll broke the silence. "Blake?"

Turning his head slowly to meet his dad's eyes, he didn't say a word.

"I wanted to talk to you about something." Mr. Knoll's voice was only a whisper.

Blake sat back in his chair to brace himself for whatever it might be. "Ok."

He took a struggled breath. "I... I'm sorry."

Mr. Knoll's voice was broken and Blake wasn't sure he heard him right. Everything inside him stopped. "What?"

His dad dropped his eyes and seemed to be struggling to find the words. "I'm sorry... for everything." He turned to look up at Blake. Blake stared at his dark eyes and saw something he'd never seen before, regret.

"I'm sorry for the horrible things I put you and your mom through because of my selfishness. I was a horrible person, the worst I know." Mr. Knoll paused to catch his breath. "The night you and your mom left, I lost my mind, not because I had lost the best things that ever happened to me, but because I had to face myself alone." He paused again. "I couldn't look at you or your mom and blame you for all the things I thought were wrong. I knew you had just left for training and so I thought I could convince your mom to come back since you would be leaving later that year. I looked for her day and night."

Blake could only stare at his dad. No matter how bad he didn't want to relive the past he sat quietly as his dad continued.

"After weeks of searching I finally found her at the grocery store. When I saw her it wasn't joy or relief that I felt, it was anger. I waited for her to come out and get in her car. I followed her to that run down little apartment you found for her."

Blake flinched as he said it. It had been all they could find. He was only nineteen and fresh out of high school, he only had a small amount of money to offer for them to move in with one of his mother's friends. He hated the thought of them staying there in that environment but it seemed better than at home, especially since he was set to leave in a few weeks. He couldn't just leave her alone to take punches. He steadied his breathing to help fade the pounding in his ears.

"I forced her to come with me. She told me she wouldn't but I made her. That's when she told you she was moving back home." Mr. Knoll's eyes struggled to hold back the tears, but he didn't look away from Blake. Blake swallowed hard remembering when his mom called to tell him she couldn't live in that small apartment and that she was going to go back home. He'd begged her not to. He was so angry with his dad, but couldn't do anything about it living several states away.

"Things went back to normal. You were finishing basic, I was drinking, and she was taking pills. She was miserable and filled with worry but I didn't care to acknowledge it. It made me angrier. I blamed you." His voice caught as he said it. "I blamed you because you gave your mom hope that she could escape. I couldn't. I was trapped in my own personal hell. I wasn't about to let her leave again."

Blake felt his anger try to regain ground in his heart. The pounding picking up speed in his head.

"You made your decisions for noble causes and wanted to protect your mom. I was so mad at you. I wanted to make you suffer like I was suffering." A tear ran down his dad's cheek. "I shouldn't have ever threatened you with hurting Melissa. She was the person you loved and who loved you back. No father should ever want to hurt their child like that." He took another breath. "I can't justify why I wanted to hurt you so bad. I was really messed up inside. Every night must've been a nightmare for your mother." His inhale was shaky that time. "Then one night, I came home from the bar like most every night and the house was silent. I called out to her and she didn't answer. I went down the hall and into the bed..."

"DON'T!" Blake held his hand up. Dropping his head, he blinked his eyes dry. He didn't need to hear anymore. He knew the rest. He raised his eyes to see something he had never seen before. His dad's face was shining from the flood of tears running down his face. Blake felt the ache surge in his chest. "Why are you telling me this?"

His dad took a few deep shaky breaths. "One of the nurses here has been coming in and praying with me every morning. She gave me a Bible and read some to me." His voice caught trying to inhale deeply. "I know I can't change the past and I don't deserve the kindness you've shown me the past weeks, but I want you to know that I've asked God to forgive me and I believe He has. I'm hoping you will find a way to forgive me too."

He never thought he would ever hear his dad apologize. Like his dad, Blake had found prayer in his own way while in the service. Letting go was a major part in how Blake had coped with the things he had seen. Because of that, he didn't struggle with those demons that could easily slip a noose around his neck. Hearing his dad say that he had basically done the same thing was shocking. Forgiving him would be the hardest thing Blake would ever do. Could he really do what he was being asked?

As if he could see the battle going on in Blake, Mr. Knoll spoke again. "I know that I don't have much time left and I've been thinking about my treatment."

Blake looked surprised and grateful that he wouldn't have to be the one to bring it up. "What did you decide?"

Mr. Knoll's chest rose and fell hard with the weight of his decision. "I'm going to stop treatment. It's time."

"Are you sure?" Blake questioned.

Mr. Knoll mustered up a strong voice. "I've done the last thing I knew I needed to do, which was talk to you." Looking down at the tubes in his arm. "Chemo makes me feel sick and tired. I know that Dr. Jackson said it isn't effective any more so I want to spend my last days without treatment, however long that is."

Staring at his dad's tear stained face, Blake believed he was a changed man. Seeing him cry and hearing him acknowledge the pain he caused in the past was proof of that.

"Dad," Blake reached out and took his boney cold hand. "Thank you for what you said about me, mom, and Melissa."

Nodding his head, Mr. Knoll blinked heavy and struggled to hold his eyes open. Patting his hand Blake leaned in, "I'm going to let you get some rest. We'll talk more later."

After closing the room door behind him, Blake pressed his back against it. He still needed some time to think about everything his dad had said. The shuffle of feet reminded him he needed to find Dr. Jackson. He asked the woman at the desk to call him and soon Dr. Jackson met him at the desk a few minutes later.

"I have dad's answer about treatment."

Dr. Jackson clasped his hands at his waist. "Ok. What are his wishes?"

"He wants to stop. He seems to be ok with what that means for him." Blake dropped his shoulders.

"I will make note of it and visit with him in a little bit. Remember Blake, it will still get worse as his body succumbs to the cancer. We will do what we can to make him comfortable."

They shook hands and the doctor retreated back to where he came from. Blake headed out to his truck and leaned back against the headrest before turning on the ignition. He needed some time to search himself and brace for the coming weeks. There was only one place he knew to go.

Chapter 20

The next four days were a whirlwind for Melissa. The day before leaving for Dallas with Cami, she took Wyatt to the aquarium, ate ice cream for dinner, and practiced baseball. She hated leaving him for three days, but was excited for some girl time too. The bachelorette getaway had been so much fun. They got to embarrass Cami several times by way of a mechanical bull, a karaoke stage, and a comedy show. Melissa was so happy she went, even though she missed Wyatt like crazy. Among all the craziness, Melissa's mind couldn't stay away from Blake. The truth was she missed him. They had texted a few times while she was gone which made Melissa happy. He hadn't completely shut her out which was a relief. Her guilt was a heavy black cloak she had never been able to take off.

Melissa picked up the scattered pencils on the floor that were spilled in the students' rush out to eat lunch. She was going to have to clean up quickly in order to head over to Cami's to work on last minute wedding details. They had care packages for family members staying at the hotel to make and they needed to print out the programs and place cards. Melissa did her best to do everything and be everything Cami needed.

She sat down at her desk going over the worksheets the kids had turned in before taking a break for lunch. Just then she heard a knock on the door. She looked up to see Blake holding a bag.

"Hey." Her heart leapt in her chest. "What are you doing here?"

He smiled and said, "I thought I'd stop by and see if you were hungry. I'm hoping you haven't eaten yet." He held up a plastic bag. "If you don't mind a visitor."

"Wow. No I haven't. Please come in." She moved the papers into a stack and set them aside. "I'm surprised you came by."

Blake placed the bag on the table and started unpacking it's contents. "Well, we've only text a few times while you were gone. I know that we saw each other at your Gram's birthday but we didn't really talk."

She looked down at her lap with the reminder of their fight on the 4th of July. She wasn't sure a twenty minute break would be enough to really talk to him like he wanted.

"I wanted to apologize to you about how angry I got. I mean it when I say I don't ever want to hurt you."

She nodded and said, "Thank you. I'm sorry too."

Blake smiled. He looked down at their food and said, "Uh, I thought I would bring you some of Jade's finest. A bacon cheeseburger and cheese fries."

Melissa's mouth watered. "Cami will kill me if I don't fit into my bridesmaid dress in two days. Especially if she knew you were stuffing me with some amazingly greasy food."

"I don't think you'll ever have to worry about that. This is still your favorite meal, right?"

She took a big bite and nodded. It was and she loved that he remembered. In school, she had never worried about her weight. She wasn't the thinnest or the heaviest, just average. Blake never made her feel uncomfortable in the way she looked and so they ate what they liked to eat. Of course, that was a long time ago. Now that she was older she did watch it more closely.

"You look nice." His voice was sincere as always.

"Thanks." She smiled and released an exhale trying to let the flush leave her face.

Blake looked good too. His hair was a little longer than his clean military cut when she first saw him. His face was clean shaved and he smelled amazing. The black polo fit him perfectly, the muscles in his shoulders shifted and the pull across his chest when he inhaled made her heart race. Her attraction to him was obvious and possibly more intense than when they were kids. The Blake she knew was athletic but by no means this fit. *Calm down.* She had to get a grip on herself.

She cleared her voice and asked, "How's your dad?"

"Since stopping chemo he is awake for longer. He tries to talk to me more when I'm there." He sounded bummed and looked down at his fries.

"What is it?"

Blake sighed and looked back up at her. "He can't really hold things anymore." He paused. "It's harder than I thought it would be, you know?"

Her heart broke for him. He was really hurting more than she had expected and all she wanted to do was take it all away. "Do you need anything? Can I do anything for you?"

"Not really. He's getting worse every day and I don't want to ask you to come up there with me."

She placed her hand on his forearm. "Blake, I want to do that for you if that's what you need. I'd be happy to be there."

Blake nodded and took a drink of his water. "Let's not talk about that right now."

She pulled her hand from his arm and picked up another fry. "Ok."

"How's the wedding prep coming? Tomorrow is the rehearsal dinner." Blake took another bite of his burger.

"Things are good. Cami's panicking about things and so I'm trying to go behind her and double check everything." She took a drink of her water. "But I don't want to talk about that right now either."

He straightened his back. "Alright. What would you like to talk about?"

"Well, I only have about another ten minutes until the kids come back. I know some about your service time but what else has happened? Anything exciting or unexpected? I love a good story." She took another bite of a fry.

"Just lots of traveling and missions."

She wanted more than that. "Did you ever get to be in one place, make a place a home?"

His eyes revealed more than he may have wanted her to know. There was something that flashed across them and she knew the answer must've been yes. He took a deep breath. "After some time in Europe and the Middle East, I was given some time back in the states. I hadn't expected to have a home but when I was back in North Carolina my circumstances changed."

For some reason, she felt her nerves sneaking up at what could've changed. "Did it have to do with the military?" She watched him for a moment before he caught her staring.

He sighed and put down his burger. "No."

"No?" she questioned.

"No, the change didn't have to do with the military." He paused before continuing. "About 4 years ago I met someone."

Melissa's heart sank. It shouldn't have surprise her but it did.

"Her name was Jennifer. We ended up getting really serious over the next few years that followed."

"How serious?" Melissa asked curiously and picked up another fry.

"I thought she might be someone I could marry."

Melissa's hand froze with her fry close to her mouth. "Oh, wow." She swallowed the lump in her throat. "Did you ask her?"

"No." He shook his head. "We were happy, or so I thought. I even bought a house shortly before I left for a long mission." He stopped talking and took another drink.

She watched him for a moment relieved he hadn't gotten engaged. "Do you still have the house?"

"Yes. I didn't sell it because I knew I needed something to fall back on when I got out, especially if I get this job offer."

Melissa's heart fell to the floor. He kept the house. She looked down at her food and bit the inside of her lip. She'd let herself fall more than she should. Her guard had started to drop and she was afraid now that she ran the risk of him leaving. "Have you heard anything about the job?"

"My Sergeant called a few days ago and told me that there were only two other applicants that have been sent for consideration. So, he says I have a good chance." He looked like he wanted to say something and in a way, she wished he would.

She cleared her throat. "So, what happened… with Jennifer?"

"Let's just say, while I was jumping out of airplanes she was busy shacking up with another soldier in my bed."

Melissa stared trying to read him. At first he looked angry, possibly a little hurt. Then his expression turned indifferent.

"I'm sorry, Blake," Melissa said softly.

Leaning forward and putting his elbows on the table he looked intently into her eyes. "It's for the best. She wasn't for me and now I'm glad it didn't work out."

"I can't imagine how you must've felt…", her voice trailed off.

"She was tired of waiting I suppose."

"Waiting? What do you mean?"

He sighed, "Well, I made a promise a long time ago and have made a point to keep it. I'm saving myself for marriage."

She was surprised. In today's society, it was the norm to have sex with everyone you dated or just wanted to spend the night with. Because of her religious upbringing she had made that commitment at a young age. When they started dating, Blake had supported it too. That was one of the best things about their relationship, purity.

"Don't look so surprised," he teased.

"I guess I just didn't think you were still standing by that." She flinched at how that sounded. "I'm sorry, I didn't mean for that to come across critical."

He shrugged his shoulders. "It's not a problem. We made that decision a long time ago and I just chose to honor it."

Because of me? Her heart fluttered at the thought that he might have held out for her. They could still honor each other and God. As soon as the thought came, it left. She didn't know that she viewed herself as pure anymore. She had meant to keep her promise and commitment but it had been ripped away from her. The fear that he was thinking the wrong thing about her started to return. She didn't want him to think she cheated, she never would have. She had planned on telling him this weekend after the wedding. She opened her mouth to say something when the kids came back into the room from lunch.

Blake stood and gathered up their trash. "I guess that's my cue."

She walked him to the door and stepped out into the hall out of site of the kids. "I wish we had more time to talk."

"We will this weekend. I'm glad I was able to come see you today. Thanks for talking with me." He leaned in and kissed her check softly and pulled back. His eyes drew her in closer and she couldn't stop herself.

Without thinking, Melissa closed the distance between them. She pushed up on her toes and caught his lips with her own. She tried to convey all her feelings that she hadn't been able to tell him yet through the kiss. His hand slowly cupped her face and his fingers ran around her neck into her hair. She was lost in the taste and feel of him. Then suddenly she remembered where they were. As she pulled back breathless Melissa could see Blake was pleased with her kiss. He smiled and cleared his throat. "I better let you get back to your class."

"Ok," she said with a breath.

"I'll see you tomorrow at the rehearsal dinner." He smiled, turned, and headed out of the library. Melissa sighed and turned to walk back into her waiting students.

When he kissed her, she felt like he might be falling too. She couldn't be sure. He had a lot at stake when it came to having a relationship with her again. If he was offered the job in North Carolina it would be crazy not to take it. He already had a place to live there. She didn't want him to leave. She wanted to believe he wanted to stay not because of his dad but because of her and Wyatt.

Thinking about going any length of time apart from him made Melissa's chest constrict. She was surprised at herself for boldly kissing him with no fear, and it felt good. She was beginning to imagine a future together, a place where there were no secrets, no heartache, and no fear of losing it all. The problem with this dream was that she did have secrets, she could still cause him heartache, and she could still lose him forever.

Chapter 21

The large ball room was dimmed creating a more intimate mood. There were circle tables draped in white throughout the ballroom. Each table sparked as the candlelight bounced off the crystals hanging from the tree branch centerpieces. There was light music playing along with soft conversations carrying to every corner. Blake headed to the open bar at the far wall. With drink in hand, he turned to scan the room. There was no question who it was he was looking for.

He had decided to surprise Melissa at the library yesterday and was sure glad he did. She had told him she would talk to him after the wedding about everything since she was gone most of the week. He knew she was putting him off but after their argument at the festival, he figured they both needed time to cool off. He'd been hesitant to talk about his ex-girlfriend, Jennifer. Not because he wanted to hide it from Melissa but because he was being cautious in talking about relationships. The one he wanted to talk about was being avoided. Talking about Jennifer would do him no good in trying to reconcile with Melissa. But now that he had he felt better.

"Blake!" James stood near the head table and waved him over. "Glad you're here."

Shaking his hand, Blake slapped James's shoulder. "Of course, man."

"You clean up good for black tie." James said looking over Blake.

Blake huffed, "I don't get to dress up very often. It's not my day though. Are you ready for tomorrow?"

"Crazy, isn't it? I remember seeing Cami in high school and always wishing I was a few years older so she'd give me the time of day. I guess she didn't mind the younger guy chasing after her too much."

Blake laughed. "I guess not."

James looked out toward the room. "I really am ready. Something I never thought this would happen to me. It's funny though, now I couldn't imagine my life any other way."

Smiling at the maturity in James's words, Blake shook his head in agreement. "Love looks good on you."

"Thanks, man. You know, love looks good on you too." James paused to give an accusing smile. "In fact, it always has."

Blake knew there was no point in trying to argue with James. He had been there when Blake and Melissa became best friends and saw them together their senior year of high school. If James could tell how he felt about Melissa, he hoped she knew too. They had kissed a few times and hung out some. But he wanted her to know that deep down his feelings hadn't ever changed.

"I believe there's a girl in a little black dress about to take a seat at an empty table. She probably needs some company." James tilted his head in the direction of the tables. Blake followed his lead and found the only girl he wanted to see. James slapped his shoulder and walked off to greet other guests.

He took in the sight of Melissa as he slowly made his way in her direction. Her hair was lightly curled falling over her bare shoulders. The strapless black dress highlighted her curves perfectly and ended just above her knees. She fumbled in her purse as he approached. "May I join you?"

She looked up quickly and returned his smile. "Sure."

She took his breath away. He slid out the chair and sat down next to her. "It looks great in here. You girls did great."

"That's all Cami's doing." She dropped her eyes shyly.

"I know you did more than you'll admit."

She looked back up at him. "It's Cami's wedding and her planning. She's been working a lot and I wanted to help keep her stress down. You know how she gets."

"I do. But I want you to know that I see what you did and what you do." He wanted her to know that all she does for others wasn't going unseen. "You volunteer on your summer break to help kids learn more. You help the press with anything they ask you to cover. You're a good friend. You help your sister whenever she needs it. You help Wyatt with his baseball skills. You do so much for everyone else and I don't want you to leave close to nothing for yourself."

"I do those things because it helps and makes other people happy." Her voice was strong. "Perhaps I have to give up some things for myself to do for others."

He hated to hear her say that. "Perhaps there's someone who would like to change that for you."

He saw the dress tug at her chest as she inhaled and released. "That someone doesn't understand the things I've gone through to make me that way."

Her defensiveness made him angry. He was just trying to give her a compliment and let her know he saw her for all she was. Her never ending support to others and love to help them was uplifting. She was the one who still hadn't told him about what happened. He had done his best to not pressure her or let it cause problems between them. So, why was she blaming him for not understanding? He didn't want there to be tension between them. They had started getting close again and he didn't want her to start pulling away.

Blake tried to keep the bite from his voice. "That's not his fault."

Melissa's eyes narrowed slightly at him. "We're not having this conversation here, Blake. We agreed to after the wedding."

Blake had agreed. "Once again you're dodging the very thing that tore us apart. I said I'd wait until this weekend and I will. But I don't understand what I said that has created this tension. That's not what I want and I hope it's not what you want either."

Melissa's eyes dropped to the candles in the center of the table. "Blake, I don't want that either. There's just a lot on my mind."

"Ok." He decided to back off. Now wasn't the time or place to have an argument. He better change the subject. "How's Wyatt?"

He could see the insecurity roll off her shoulders as she sat back in her chair. "He's good. Not sure he's ready to be all dressed up tomorrow." She looked over to him sitting at a table with another young boy. "He's been hanging out with one of James's little cousins today."

"That's great. He's making friends who'll end up being family."

She simply nodded and looked back out across the room. Blake wanted to say more but some of the other bridesmaids took their seats at the table. The dinner was about to start and Blake stood to excuse himself and take his seat with the other ushers. "I'll talk to you later."

Melissa nodded and said, "Ok."

Throughout the dinner lots of friends and family got up to share personal speeches for Cami and James. The atmosphere was light and fun. Blake couldn't help but sneak looks across the room at Melissa, who was laughing and chatting with the other bridesmaids. Every so often he'd catch her looking back at him. He prayed she'd heard what he said about taking time for herself. She was special and should be appreciated. He hoped she would allow him the chance to make her feel that way.

******

The dinner was beautiful. The happy couple were all smiles and the room was full of music and laughs all night. Melissa brushed out a wrinkle in one of the lace table clothes and stepped back to look one last time. She wanted to make sure everything was ready for Cami's big day tomorrow. Melissa was very excited for them and couldn't wait to share the day with her big sister. Getting married was a beautiful thing and she was happy that Cami had found her happily ever after.

Melissa draped her dress over her arm, thankful that she brought a change of clothes for after the party. Wyatt was stretched across several chairs sound asleep. She nudged him awake, "Time to go, sweetie. Let's get out to the car."

She held his hand and they left the building. Wyatt was so sleepy that he was shuffling his feet over the gravel. "We're almost there. Just a little bit furth—" Her breath caught in her throat.

The parking lot was deserted except for two vehicles. Blake was leaning against the passenger side of his truck parked next to her car. His white button down shirt was untucked and the top button undone where his black tie had been. After her slow approach, she stepped around him headed toward her back door. Her arm brushed against him slightly, sending chills all over her body.

Melissa helped Wyatt buckle into his booster seat and then shut the door. He instantly snuggled up against the window and fell back asleep. She turned to face Blake. "You waited for me?"

Blake slid both hands in his front pockets. "I wanted to see you before tomorrow." He sighed and said, "Melissa, I'm sorry if I upset you earlier."

A pain twisted in her chest. No matter what she did she fell deeper into a hole of regret and guilt. There was no reason to have gotten defensive with Blake. She'd been thinking a lot about how much she wanted to be with him and worrying about the conversation they needed to have. When he mentioned that she left little for herself it upset her. Though she loved the thought that she was special, Melissa didn't consider herself worthy of that.

Her shoulders dropped. "I'm not mad at you, Blake. I know it seemed that way but it goes deeper than that." She wanted Blake to reach out and hold her, to feel safe in his warm arms. But he remained in place. "Do I *want* to feel special? Yes. Do I *want* to be given the chance to have everything I've ever wanted? Of course, it would be a dream." It was true, she did. "But I have to disagree that I deserve that."

Blake straightened his back and began to speak, "Mel—"

"I don't," she cut him off. "You were the person that meant more to me than anything else in the whole world. I thought that not involving you in my nightmare was best for you."

Blake's shoulders dropped.

"And with trying to do what I thought was right, I hurt you. Probably more than I could ever imagine. And I don't deserve your forgiveness." She could feel the tears trying to break free but she pushed on. "Blake, you're the only person I've ever given my heart to. I would sacrifice everything in order to give you happiness. I'm terrified because..." She took a shaky breath. "Because I still love you. I love you and yet I know my heart may shatter, but I feel like I still mean something to you too. And if that's true..." The tears break free. "If that's true, I don't want to hurt you again."

"You love me?" Blake asked on a breath.

Melissa saw the light in his eyes. "Yes."

Blake took one step and his lips found hers. He cupped her face with his hands and she slid her hands around his waist. His kiss was smooth and passionate, as if he was savoring every second. She felt desire, longing, passion, and love. She had never been kissed like that. It was more than she'd ever experienced with Blake before. Her cheeks were damp in a blend of both their tears. His lips ventured from her lips to her cheeks and then just below her jawline. Blake's kisses slowly lost their hunger and became tender again. He made his way back up her cheek and landed one last kiss on her lips. He slowly pulled back, staying close enough that she could feel his breath brush across her face and down her neck. His thumbs swiped away their shared tears.

"I've been wanting to kiss you like that for years," Blake's voice raspy and as he caught his breath. "I'm done trying to act like we are just old friends who kiss to comfort each other."

She leaned back enough for his hands to release her face. That's what she wanted too. She wanted to believe they could have all those things. Melissa dropped her eyes down to the ground and wrapped her arms around her stomach. "Blake, I want to believe that we can have that, but I don't know if it's possible. I've hurt you and I keep hurting you."

Blake placed his hands on her shoulders, his voice was strong and full of intent. "Don't do this. Don't close yourself off from me again."

"I don't want to, Blake. I just..." Her voice quivered with nervousness again. "I just..."

"I'm done fighting this. I don't want to argue. I want..." He stopped as though he caught himself before finishing.

"Blake?" she whispered.

He closed the gap between them again and cupped her face, sliding his fingers below her ears. "You. I want you. I love you, Melissa." His body shuddered as he inhaled. "I. Love. You. End of story. I want everything that comes with you, even without knowing what all that includes." Searching her eyes, he continued, "You said you love me. Can you look at me and tell me you don't want to be with me?"

She couldn't tell him no. In fact, her feelings were stronger now than when they were kids. Could she look beyond the unknown of what their future would look like? To be with him she'd have to. Willing the air to fill her lungs she exhaled and said, "I can't."

A smile spread across his face and he kissed her forehead softly. He dropped his chin and pressed his forehead against hers. "Melissa, please don't push me away. Let me love you."

He broke through her last line of defense. For the first time in years, she was making her mind up not to worry about her past. She didn't want to doubt that she was worthy to be loved. He wanted to be with her and she wanted to be with him. Could that be enough?

The grip her hands had across her stomach faltered. His arms took their place and pulled her flush with him. No matter what her fears had been, she accepted his embrace. Feeling his firm chest against her cheek, his heart beat was strong. A heart she knew was the only one she'd ever loved. Blake wanted her. He loved her. The truth was she missed being able to show him she loved him too. Now if only he still felt that way once she told him everything.

Chapter 22

In the surrounding trees, dangling strings of lights danced over the large pond creating the perfect backdrop for the wedding ceremony. A mixture of white and pink flowers lined the center aisle along the uniformed white chairs. A combination of interlaced branches and flowers created the arch at the end of the isle. Cami wanted an outdoor ceremony and a beautiful banquet hall for the reception and they found the perfect location west of Shaw Creek.

When Cami walked down the aisle, Melissa had never seen James smile so big. Cami was an absolute vision in her bridal gown. From the vows to the songs played it was a beautiful testament to their love. Wyatt did such a good job to stand still throughout the whole ceremony. He looked so grown up in his little tux and gelled hair.

The reception hall was full of life and music and everything was perfectly in place the way Melissa had left it last night. The other bridesmaids at her table were laughing and enjoying light conversation. She spotted Blake across the room visiting with some friends. He was dressed in his black tux and white button down dress shirt. The memory of him kissing her last night made the heat in her chest rise up her neck. He caught her looking at him and she matched his smile. She hadn't spoken to him since they said their good byes in the parking lot. She had thought about him all night and again when she woke up. She felt like a teenager again. He winked at her from across room and she couldn't help but blush.

Wyatt plopped down between Melissa and Gram and he started fidgeting with the collar of his white button down shirt. Melissa was so proud that he walked down the aisle and stood in front of the crowd without any problems. For a seven year old, he maintained a great level of obedience through the ceremony and pictures but now Wyatt was rubbing his eyes.

"Are you sleepy, honey?" Melissa asked patting his back.

He looked up at her and nodded. She kissed the side of his head and said, "We'll be headed home in just a little bit. Thank you for being such a good boy. I know Aunt Cami really appreciated what you did."

After finishing dinner, Wyatt joked at their table with Aly and Aunt Sarah. Melissa excused herself from the table and made her way to the edge of the dance floor. Where she saw Jade with a big smile as she danced with Melissa's cousin Luke. Jade made eye contact with her and shrugged and Melissa shook her head in amusement. If she didn't know any better, both of them were pretty smitten. Her eyes fell on Cami as she glided across the floor with James. The way they looked at each other, it was as if there was no one else in the room. At the start of another slow song, several couples joined the newlyweds. Suddenly, she felt a familiar pair of fingers lace her own and pull her toward the dance floor.

"Dance with me?" Blake's voice was soft and she couldn't resist it.

She followed him out onto the wood floor. He spun her around and pulled her toward him settling in with his arms around the small of her back. He kissed her forehead and inhaled as if soaking in her perfume. She relaxed letting her feet follow his slow steps.

"You're a great dancer," Melissa said.

"Thanks. You're a great partner." Blake spun her out and back in.

She leaned closer to Blake's chest, inhaling his rustic cologne and feeling the rhythm of his heartbeat. His lips brushed her forehead and she appreciated his tender touch. She wanted to memorize this moment and hold onto it forever. He was sincere and tender, yet strong and bold. She was happy, genuinely happy. Everyone else faded and all she wanted was to stay right there with Blake. The next phrase of the song caught her attention.

You've given me hope
You've helped me see
That I'm more than I thought I could be
You've given me a chance
You've broken through my wall
I stand here not scared at all

That's exactly what Blake was doing for her.

Blake leaned back and looked at her. "Do you want to go outside with me?"

She nodded. He once again laced their fingers and lead her outside. They pushed past the tables until they broke through the double doors to the warm summer night. There was no one out by the pond where the ceremony had been. The sky was clear and the moon bright. Lightening bugs danced in the air to the crickets' melody. Melissa fumbled with a few of her loose curls as they sat together on one of the outer square bales near the pond.

"You're beautiful you know that?" Blake took her hand from her curls and kissed just above the knuckles.

Blushing, Melissa straightened her back and said, "You look handsome, as always."

"Thanks." He winked at her.

Melissa linked her arm through his and rested her head on his shoulder, just like they used to. They spent several minutes not saying anything, just being together. Her mind wondered back to sitting with Blake in the sunflowers under the old oak tree. The feelings she had for Blake were different from when they were kids. She felt young again and it was amazing to feel important to him. Sure, Gram was kind to her and Wyatt was always giving her flowers and kisses, but to feel valued and seen by a man was something she wasn't sure she would feel again. She loved how Blake was passionate and talked openly with her. Then Blake sighed heavy.

Melissa pulled him tighter to her, hugging his arm. He looked down at her and she could see the longing in his eyes. "What are you thinking?" she asked.

Blake smiled and said, "I'm glad you're here with me." He took a deep breath. "I feel like you're still scared to open up to me."

She dropped her eyes. "Blake—"

"You don't ever have to worry about opening up to me, Mel. I want to take this journey with you. I always have. It's been a lonely road but it's amazing to think it doesn't have to be anymore."

Her heart melted at his words. As he lifted her chin with his index finger, she felt the tears break free off her lids and fall down her cheeks. His eyes were soft and understanding. He leaned in and kissed her lips so tenderly. Blake's touch was intoxicating. She pulled at his shirt, taking their kiss deeper. He broke from her and ran his lips down her jaw line finding the tender spot just below her ear. Goosebumps rose from his touch and she could feel his pulse under her palm. Then his body tensed and his kisses lost their hunger as he slowly put on the breaks.

Trying to catch his breath, Blake leaned his forehead against hers and said, "Wow."

She smiled knowing he was just as winded as she was. "Blake, I'm ready to tell…"

"BLAKE!" They both jumped at the sound of his name. Turning, they saw James running out toward them.

Blake stood up quickly leaving Melissa sitting alone on the hay bale. "What is it?"

"It's your dad," James tried to catch his breath. "The cancer center called the reception hall."

Blake's face went white. "What's wrong? Is he ok?"

Melissa stood slowly nervous to know the answer. Something must be wrong for them to call.

"They didn't say exactly. They just said you need to come up there. It's an emergency."

Blake shook his head and started around James when Melissa grabbed his arm. "Let me come with you."

He nodded and she gripped his hand as they bolted back into the building. She grabbed her bag from one of the changing rooms and ran back to Wyatt and Aly.

Melissa knelt down in front of Wyatt. "Sweetie, I'm going to go help Blake."

"You look scared, Mommy."

She ran her fingers through Wyatt's hair. "I'm ok. When our friends need help we've got to do what we can to be there for them. Blake's my friend and I'm going to try to help him." Melissa looked at Aly. "I'm not sure how late I'll be. Can you take him home?"

Aly nodded, "Of course."

"Here are my car keys." She pulled them out of her bag and handed them to Aly. She turned back to Wyatt. "Aunt Aly is going to take you home in just a little bit. Can you be good for her?"

"Yes, Mommy."

"Ok." Melissa pulled Wyatt into a hug and kissed his head. "I love you. I'll see you back at home."

Melissa turned and ran toward the exit. She found Blake waiting for her at the door. He looked scared and Melissa felt her stomach drop out. They hopped into his truck and pulled out of the parking lot like a race car. She was nervous to look over at him for fear that she would lose the tight grip she held on to her emotions.

Finally, she couldn't take the silence anymore. Without looking at him she asked, "How did they know how to contact you?"

Blake's voice was firm and low. "I told them I had a wedding and wasn't going to be coming by dad's today."

Melissa knew there was no need to say anything else. It wouldn't help. She looked out her window and did something she hadn't done in a long time, prayed.

God, I know I've not been as faithful as I should but I need you to hear me this time. Blake has been alone his whole life, and now that he is finally building a relationship with his dad he needs some more time. Don't take him yet. Please let us get there and let Blake see him again. Amen.

She felt a tear fall down her cheek and she quickly wiped it before Blake could notice. He was quiet the rest of the drive.

As they neared the center, Melissa snuck a look at him and saw a single tear running down his face. Regardless of what Blake said, Melissa knew his love reached far beyond just her. It reached to a father Blake once hated and it ran deeper than he'd been willing to admit until now.

Chapter 23

The hall looked the same as it always did. Nurses and doctors making their rounds and helping their patients. The weight in the air almost suffocated Blake. It didn't matter how many times he had made this walk, today the weight was heavier. Darker. Gripping Melissa's hand reassured him that she was there for him, just like when they were kids. Making this walk alone might have been more than Blake could take. The nurse caught them before they entered.

"I-Is everything ok?" Blake's voice was shaky.

"He had a close call but is stable now." She paused, hesitant to tell him more. "He has opened his eyes. We can't guarantee anything at this point."

Blake felt the air get sucked from him lungs. It was worse than the time he was caught in a sand storm in the middle east, his lungs desperate for air, but not finding any. He knew this was coming. He just wasn't ready for it to happen. "Can I see him now?"

"As you know he hasn't been able to speak much at all the past few days. I'm not sure his body is strong enough to now. We don't know if he'll wake up but if he does, he can hear you." The look in her eyes didn't hide her doubt.

Blake pushed the door open and did his best to keep his feet moving forward. He made his way to the middle of the room and looked down at the man in the hospital bed. His dad was asleep and there were more tubes than when he was there yesterday. Blake released a deep breath and walked around the bed where he took his place in the chair next to his dad's side. Melissa took the seat against the wall at the foot of the bed.

Blake could feel the bed give at the weight of his elbows but it was nothing compared to the sinking feeling in his stomach. There is no telling how long he just sat there watching his dad take shallow breaths. Their conversation last week consumed Blake's heart. Why hadn't he talked with his dad then? He felt Melissa watching as he spoke into the silence. "I should've forgiven him."

"What do you mean?" Melissa asked.

"I had a conversation with him last week and he told me everything. He told me why he did the things he did to me, to mom, and to himself." Never losing site of his father in the bed, Blake exhaled. "He asked me to forgive him and I didn't." His voice was a whisper, almost not wanting her to hear him. For a moment, he wasn't sure she had.

"Oh, Blake." Melissa slowly stood and walked over to him. She knelt down next to him and placed her hand on his arm. Her voice soft. "You can now."

He turned to look at her and saw that she had unshed tears that matched his own. "The sad thing is that after he told me everything I didn't want to forgive him. Everything I've lost in my life was a result of his actions, his decisions: my childhood, my mother, a relationship with him, and y…" He caught himself before he said anything else. "Everything I've loved."

"Everything?" Melissa's voice cracked at her question.

Blake didn't want to expose his dad's actions toward Melissa, not now. He couldn't do that to them right now. She wasn't the only one who had kept a secret from their past. There was no way to know how she would respond and this wasn't the place.

"Can you tell me?" she asked.

Telling her about his dad's threats would accomplish nothing, especially at his dad's bedside. Blake broke away from her eyes and looked back at his dad. She was a master of avoidance so she should understand. Melissa must've felt him close off because she dropped her head, stood, and made her way back to the end of the bed. Blake hated himself for being so selfish. "Melissa?"

She turned and the look in her eyes broke his heart. Everything in him wanted to jump up and tell her everything but he couldn't. "I didn't mean to be so cold. I just can't…"

"Talk to me about it." Her tone was hard as she interrupted him. He could tell she was trying to keep from getting upset. She shook her head and began to walk toward the door.

He felt anger starting to build in his chest. "Melissa, you can't say any—"

"I'm sorry," she interrupted. "I'm going to go change out of this dress." She looked at his dad. "I think you need some time alone."

Blake watched her leave the room. Just an hour ago they were completely enveloped in each other. Blake wanted nothing more than to be sitting on that hay bale again. In that moment, all the doubt he had about their relationship disappeared. Now he was sitting facing all of them head on. He looked back at his dad. Melissa was right. Even though he didn't say anything to his dad earlier, he could still forgive him now.

Blake took his dad's hand and squeezed it tight, as though trying to transfer some of his own life back into his dad. He felt the tears carve a path down his face. They were tears that he had pinned down for twenty years hoping never to show. It was a burden he tried to carry for his mother and failed. It was a burden he tried to protect Melissa from and she pushed him away. He didn't want to live like that anymore. Taking a deep breath, he was ready to talk to his dad.

"Dad?" Blake asked. "I don't know if you can hear me, but it's Blake." There was no response or proof he was awake but Blake continued. "I came as soon as they told me. I'm sorry I wasn't here today." He prayed for his voice to remain steady so he could get out all he needed to say.

"I'm sorry, Dad. I'm so sorry. When we talked the other day, I got upset. I should've done this a long time ago. I was angry with you, really angry. I blamed you for all the problems in my life, for all the heartache I faced. When you apologized, and talked to me about everything I didn't know how to take it. I had wanted to hear you say those things my whole life. When you finally did, I didn't want to hear them. The truth is, it's easier to be upset and angry than it is to forgive."

"Spending the last few months with you every day has allowed God to change my heart. Not over night by any means but I was softening to you. When I was on a mission half a world away I would think about you and mom. I would think about Melissa. I was willing to jump out of an airplane into unknown territories but not willing to do the same with the people in my life. I would risk everything in me to help a stranger or the brother fighting next to me, but I wouldn't for you."

Blake stared at his dad and then down at his hand. "Dad," Blake's voice caught and he knew this was it. He was going to lay everything from the shadows of his heart out on the hospital bed in front of him. "I forgive you. I forgive you for the words you said and for never being there for me. I forgive you for hitting mom and the way you treated her. I forgive you for...," he sucked in a breath. "...for threatening me about Melissa. I forgive you for making me feel like you could control everything in my life, including my relationship with her. I forgive you for... everything."

He pressed his forehead to the back of his dad's hand. Letting his tears run over them without judgement. All the hurt, anger, bitterness, and regret poured out over their hands dampening the bed sheets beneath. "And Dad, there's something else." Blake lifted his head to look at his dad again. "I wasn't just angry with you. I hated you. When I found out that you were sick I didn't want to come. I didn't want to think about feeling sorry for you or sad that you were sick but I did. And I'm glad I came. I could've handle things differently. I need to ask you to forgive me too."

The moment Blake finished talking he felt everything lift off of him. He felt that if he let go of his dad's hand he would float out of his chair. A peace that he couldn't explain washed over his soul and relieved the gripping pain in his chest. Blake went to loosen his grip when he felt his dad's hand tighten. He leaned forward hoping he hadn't just imagined it. "Dad? Can you hear me?"

Almost instantly his dad squeezed his hand. Joy burst inside Blake's chest and he could only hope that God had allowed his dad to hear all he said. "D-did you hear me talking to you, Dad?"

This time Mr. Knoll gripped tighter and longer than before. Blake knew then his dad heard everything. He leaned his forehead once again on their joined hands and released even more, more than he ever thought he could. Blake sat there returning his dad's squeeze until it slowly let up and went limp again. He loosened his grip and leaned back in his chair. He thanked God for giving him the chance to see his dad again, to talk to him, and to forgive him.

Looking up again he spotted the small painting across the room. *Melissa.* He had his own beautiful girl who loved walking through sunflowers and he needed to find her.

Blake walked around for a little while and finally spotted Melissa sitting in the commons area on the first floor. She was messing with her phone as he approached. "There you are."

She looked up at him but didn't smile. Tucking her phone back in her pocket she said, "Yeah, I walked around after I changed and settled on this bench." She fidgeted with a hang nail and continued, "I'm sorry I got mad, Blake. I had no right to get mad at you, especially with what I've put you through."

Blake couldn't argue with that but was happy to hear her say it.

Her eyes softened again. "Is everything ok?"

He slid his hands in his pockets. "Dad squeezed my hand when I talked to him."

"Blake, that's wonderful." After a few seconds, Melissa dropped her eyes back to the ground.

Blake hated that there was distance between them as a result of everything left unsaid. He grabbed her hands and pulled her up into his arms. Thankfully, she returned his embrace. Pressing his lips against her hair, he inhaled her scent which surpassed the abundant amount of hairspray. "I'm sorry our time got cut short at the wedding."

"It's ok. I'm glad I was able to come with you." She tightened her arms around him.

"Me too." He held her for several moments before stepping back to look at her. "Let's get you home. I'm going to come back up in the morning."

"It's ok. Aly called and said Wyatt wasn't feeling well. I need to get back to him so I called Jade. She just text me and told me she was parking the car."

"Oh, ok." Blake leaned down to pick up her bag. "Let me walk you out?"

Melissa took his extended hand. "Ok."

They walked through the lobby and out toward the crosswalk to the parking lot where Jade was waving from across the drive and Melissa waved back.

"Mel, I can't tell you how much I appreciate you coming with me. I just wish—"

Melissa pulled him into a hug. "Blake, you need to be here. I'm going to go home and check on Wyatt. I can come by in the morning and bring you anything you need."

Blake leaned back to see her face. The most beautiful caramel eyes he'd ever seen held such compassion and longing with a hint of sadness. "Are we ok?"

She squeezed his waist with her arms. "You don't need to worry about us right now." Before he could respond to her she kissed his cheek and took her bag. "Remember, call me if you need anything."

Blake nodded. "Drive safe."

As Blake watched her leave, he felt like all the foundation they'd been building was cracked. He saw it in her eyes before she left his dad's room. He never wanted her to feel like he was closing himself off from her, especially since she was still doing that to him. But now the important thing was to be there for his dad.

When he arrived back at his dad's room, Blake pressed his forehead against the closed door and his hand was frozen on the knob. *I don't know how to do this, Lord. I need your help.* With that prayer, he took a deep breath and pushed through the door.

Chapter 24

It had been a week since Mr. Knoll's memorial service. The service was very small. Aside from Blake, Melissa, and her family there were only a handful of other people, most were from the cancer center. Mr. Knoll had no one other than Blake. The service was very well done by the funeral director. Blake seemed to have a peace as everyone headed to the cemetery behind the funeral home. He smiled at Melissa and had somehow kept himself together throughout the day. They laid Mr. Knoll to rest next to Blake's mom. Melissa did her best to stay strong in support of Blake but made sure not to push herself on him. Gram was a big help offering wise words to him and always carrying herself with grace and tenderness.

Melissa tried her best to be supportive and help Blake with anything he needed. Though he wasn't cold, Blake had wanted to spend time alone, which Melissa respected. He had to deal with his dad's estate and begin to settle any debts. She spent most of her days completing the last week of tutoring at the summer youth program and spending extra time with Wyatt. They practiced his baseball and took walks through the sunflower field. If Blake needed anything she would make sure to fulfill those needs.

When Melissa and Wyatt reached the edge of the sunflowers, the street came into view. She saw Blake's truck backed into his drive. Melissa missed him and knew she needed to talk to him. Since their time together at Cami's wedding, the distance had only seemed to grow between them. They had talked every day but their conversation was only surface level.

"Wyatt, I think I'm going to check on Blake."

"Ok, I'm going to show Gram the rock I found!" Wyatt turned and ran up to the front door.

Once she saw he was safely inside, Melissa turned toward Blake's house. She paused just outside his door. It was time. She had to be honest and tell him everything. She knew she wanted to be with Blake and in order for that to happen there could be no secrets. Taking a deep breath, she pushed the doorbell.

When the door opened, Melissa felt everything inside her turn to mush. It appeared Blake hadn't cut his hair since he'd been home. It was messy and starting to curl at the ends. He had on a white t-shirt that highlighted his broad shoulders and chest. His dark sport shorts hung low on his hips. Melissa felt the butterflies form in her stomach and she knew she wanted Blake. He was the only guy she'd ever wanted.

"Hey," he said with a smile.

"Hey. I wanted to come see you." Melissa smiled.

Blake stepped back to allow her in. "I'm glad you did."

She walked past him to the living room and took a seat on the sofa.

"Would you like a bottle of water?" Blake walked past her toward the kitchen.

"Yes. Thank you."

Blake retrieved two bottles, crossed the room, and handed her one. "It's getting too hot out there." Blake took a seat next to her.

Their legs were only centimeters apart and Melissa could feel the warmth from his body. She wanted nothing more than to kiss him until she couldn't think. But there was something she needed to do first.

"How did your last week of tutoring go?" Blake asked.

"Good. I think all the kids I worked with will do great next year. It's exciting to see them improve." She took a drink of water.

Blake nodded and leaned his head back against the sofa, closing his eyes. Melissa looked down at her hands and she began twisting the strings of her bracelet nervously. The intertwined colors didn't even compare to the knot in her stomach. Blake placed his hand over hers and looked down at her. The desire in his eyes made her feel like he wanted to kiss her too.

Blake's ringtone blasted through the room and made her jump. He leaned forward, looked at who it was, and returned it to the coffee table. He placed his hand over hers and sat back closer to her this time.

"Someone you don't want to talk to?" she asked.

He sighed. "My Sergeant."

Melissa knew the only reason for the calls would be regarding the job opportunity he was waiting to hear about. "What does he want?"

Blake shifted in his seat uncomfortably and Melissa knew it wasn't what she wanted to hear. Still, she needed to know. "Blake?"

Blake looked at her for a moment and then said, "He called me earlier this week, after dad's funeral, and said they wanted to make me a job offer. It's the veteran specialist assistant job I told you about in North Carolina."

Melissa exhaled slowly. She wasn't surprised he got the job. That meant he would be leaving. She cleared her throat and tried to sound happy for him. "That's great." She looked down at their joined hands and began rubbing her thumb across his. "When do you leave?"

"I haven't given them an answer yet. That's why he keeps calling. I told him about dad and they said they'd give me until Monday."

Melissa looked back up at his ocean blue eyes. "That's in three days."

"Yeah," Blake said on a breath. "That's the first time he's called me since offering me the job. I can't answer him yet."

Melissa wanted to tell him not to do it. But the fact that he didn't answer yet meant he was really considering it. She was terrified that she'd allowed herself to believe they could be together. She came over here to tell him everything and now she felt as though the little hope she'd been holding onto could still be extinguished.

******

Blake had been worried about talking to Melissa about the job offer. He really didn't know what he wanted to do. In a way, he didn't think he'd get it and there would be no problem. He wanted to be with her and was willing to turn that offer down to do so. But he was running out of time and waiting for Melissa to be honest with him wasn't really an option anymore.

"Is everything ok?" Blake asked worried.

"No," her voice sounded defeated as she fiddled with her bracelet.

"I want to talk to you about this. I'm not going to answer him until we've talked." He squeezed her hand, willing her to look at him. "Melissa?"

"Blake, I want to talk to you about everything. That's the reason I came over here, really." She stood up and started to pace. Blake stayed where he was trying his best to give her a moment to collect herself.

"I want to ask you something first. At the hospital, the night of Cami's wedding, you told me that you don't ever want me to close off from you."

He knew where this was going. "I'm sorry. I know you were just trying to help and be there for me. There were so many things going through my mind and I couldn't process them fast enough."

"I understand that." She stepped back creating more space between them. "Blake, I'm the one that needs to apologize. I've been doing that to you for years. I didn't really know how it made you feel until now and I'm sorry. I can't tell you how sorry I am."

Blake didn't know what to say. He couldn't disagree with her. So, he simply nodded.

"You said that everything you've lost was because of him. I know you almost said that included me. How does it?"

Blake didn't want her to know but he didn't want there to be any secrets with her, at least on his part. It clearly upset her but he couldn't find his voice or the will power to talk about it again.

"I want to know. Whatever it is."

Blake dropped his eyes to the ground and pressed his elbows into his knees. Telling Melissa about his dad's threats and plans to find her shouldn't bother him. Nothing had come from it but he didn't know how she would react.

"Ok," her tone got a little stronger. "I want to know. You *can't* share your pain with me or you *won't*?"

Her question irritated him. "I can't share?" He stood to his feet. "Ok maybe there is something that I need to tell you but I've been waiting for eight years for you to share your pain with me, if nothing more than to just be honest with me." His voice was angrier than he wanted. "I'm not the only one holding back."

"I've been wanting to tell you and came close a couple of times since you've been back. That's why I'm here, Blake." He could hear the slight shake in her voice.

"I'm going to say what you just said to me." He felt his frustration rising in his chest again. "It's been eight years. It's been two months since reconnecting. And *you* still can't share your pain with me."

"Blake, I'm here!"

He shook his head in disgust. "Then why was the first question about me and what I'm hiding?" Her head dropped and she wrapped her arms around her center. She still couldn't say it? Blake was done tip toeing around. "I've been willing to wait and haven't forced you to tell me. I've even gotten close to you again. You're the one who keeps dodging the truth. I've been patient regardless of how selfish you've been."

When Melissa's head snapped up he could see tears fill her eyes. "It was hard to talk about what happened to anyone, Blake. It's not like I can just shut that part of me off. I've lived with it every day for the past eight years! The guilt. The regret. It haunts me. There's never been a day that's gone by when I haven't thought about it."

"You didn't have to! All I've ever wanted was for you to tell me the truth, to be honest with me. I want to believe that this is something we can move past, together. But I need to know. I have to know." The desperation pressed against his chest harder than any tactical vest ever had.

She ran her hands through her hair. Her shoulders shuddered and he could tell she was trying to get her emotions under control. Looking him in the eye, she said, "Ok."

He hadn't meant for them both to get so upset at the start of this conversation, but he couldn't stop it now.

"I went to college just like we planned. Jade and I got one of the suites and so that meant we needed two other roommates. Samantha stayed closed off from all of us. We only saw her when we were in our suite. Amber was the other roommate. We didn't know that much about her but we soon found out that she was a party animal, to put it lightly. About a month after school started, she convinced us all to go out with her to one of the parties off campus. Jade and I thought it would be good to meet more people and so I offered to be their designated driver."

She exhaled and her shoulders shuddered. "There were lots of people there. So, I stayed as close to Jade as I could but she struck up a conversation with some guy she just met. I sat silently just watching everyone around me. A guy came by and offered me a drink since I was sitting alone. My sheltered life hadn't even made me think about what could've happened to me by accepting what looked like punch. I was young and naïve. I didn't know that it had been spiked." She looked down at the ground as if getting a handle and then looked back up at him.

Blake felt his pulse pick up as he started to realize where this story was going.

"I started to feel funny and things became blurry. I didn't know what was really going on. I got up to try and find Jade. We needed to find Amber and get back to our suite, but I fell against the wall. Some guy came over to ask me if I was ok. I don't even know who he was. He told me he'd help me find my friend and before I knew it I was in a back bedroom and the lights were off." The tears started to spill out of her eyes and Blake's heart stopped at what she was getting ready to admit.

"I don't know much about what happened other than it hurt, a lot. I couldn't move and felt like I was suffocating from the weight of him on top of me." She wiped her face. "When he was finished, I just laid there for a long time, alone. Jade asked some people if they had seen me and went looking for me. She's the one that found me in the back bedroom. She helped me out of the bed and we left the house. Then she took me to the hospital."

Blake stood frozen by shock, anger, and worry. Sure, he'd wondered if she'd had a one night stand but he never thought about rape. *She'd been raped?* He took a step toward her but she held a hand up.

"I'm not done." She swallowed hard. "I was going to come to your graduation. I knew that you'd have no one there and I desperately wanted to see you and tell you what had happened. A few weeks before, I was sick every day. I went to the doctor hoping that it wasn't the flu because I needed to see you. That's when I found out I was pregnant." She wiped her face. "That's when I made the decision not to tell you what happened."

"Melissa, why?" His heart was broken to think that she didn't want him to know.

"Because I was embarrassed. I was terrified. I didn't know how you'd react." She shifted on her feet.

All Blake wanted to do was wrap his arms around her and never let the nightmare hold her captive again, but he stayed rooted to the floor.

"People called me horrible things: slut, whore, trash, used. I know people were whispering when I sat next to Gram in church with my big swollen belly and no wedding ring. Just like I know what you must've thought when you first saw Wyatt."

Blake wanted to correct her. "Mel—"

"It's ok, Blake. I'm not mad about that. If I'm honest it's what I would've thought too." She sighed. "I wasn't going to terminate the pregnancy because I don't believe in that. I thought it would be better to spare you from the mess my life had become. We'd planned a whole future and then my future changed. You deserved to be free from that burden. I was afraid you wouldn't want me." She dropped her head. "I'm used and damaged. Why would you want a baby that wasn't yours?"

He took two steps and cupped her face. "Melissa," She closed her eyes and tried to turn her face away. "Look at me." He needed her to hear him. She lifted her eyes to meet his. "You are *not* used. You are *not* damaged. Don't you dare believe that. What happened to you was not your fault. You are worth more than being tossed to the side and forgotten, so is Wyatt."

Blake guided her over to the sofa and pulled her down onto his lap. She curled up against him and he held her tight. He would hold her as long as she'd let him. Her body shook as she let all her tears soak his shirt. He didn't want her to believe for a minute more that she wasn't worth it, especially to him. Knowing the truth now, the things she had told him before started to make sense. No, he didn't agree with the way she went about it, but now he could sympathize with her. He could love her as she continued to heal. He could pour love, acceptance, and value over her every day. Blake knew that whatever happened, he would do everything in his power to love her with everything he had. He didn't care how long it took him but he was going to hold her until she believed it.

Chapter 25

Melissa clung to Blake's white shirt feeling his strong and steady heart beat but afraid that if she released it he'd disappear forever. What surprised her more than anything was that Blake wasn't mad. He'd been holding her for close to twenty minutes letting her cry. She'd never felt more vulnerable and yet protected at the same time. She pushed up to look into his face and she saw what she always wanted. Love.

"I'm sorry that I got upset."

He kissed her forehead. "I don't want you to ever feel like you can't share your struggles with me. I especially want to know about the things that haunt you. Your pain is mine. I'm here, Mel." She nodded and he swiped the loose tear from her cheek.

Melissa tucked herself back into his chest. Now that she told him everything Melissa felt better. It was as if all that pent-up fear was for nothing. Aly was right. Blake had surprised her and she only wished that she hadn't let her fear keep her from him eight years ago.

Blake sighed heavily. "I need to tell you something too. You're not the only one who has a secret."

Melissa's gut clenched. She had a feeling this had to do with her question about his dad. She leaned back and looked into his sad face. "Tell me," she whispered.

"Remember when we were in the hospital room with dad and I told you that he talked to me and apologized?" She nodded. "Then I said that he was the reason I had lost everything important to me in my life."

"Yes," she answered.

"Well, when I didn't hear from you and you didn't come to my graduation I knew something must be wrong. I didn't know what to think, honestly. Once I got settled at my first base I knew I had to get ahold of you. Of course, I couldn't come to see you for a while so I tried to call. I tried your cell phone but the number was no good. I tried Gram's house and talked to her and she said that she couldn't answer for you. When I asked to talk to you, she told me that you'd told her that you didn't want to talk to me but that she'd tell you that I called."

Melissa dropped her shoulders. She hated that she'd made that decision. "That's my fault. I told her what to say if you ever called. She was just doing what I asked. I was still pregnant at that time. She did tell me that you tried to contact me."

Blake tucked a loose hair behind her ear. "I know that now. But I was in a panic and I became desperate to find out. So, the following summer I got to come home for a few days. I wanted to find you."

"They told me," she said.

"Gram and Julie let me come in to visit with them. They wouldn't tell me where you were and said you were going through something. When I tried to protest, they told me you'd chosen not to tell me. Gram kissed my cheek and apologized when I left. I tried Jade too but she said the same thing. I was running out of time and decided to ask dad about you. I chose not to stay with him and just got a hotel for the weekend. So, when I showed up at his door step he was surprised and let's just say I didn't get a hero's welcome."

Melissa's heart sank. Not only did Blake have to graduate alone but all the people who should've loved and supported him turned him away, especially her.

"Dad was really messed up. He was still mad at me for trying to get mom out of there when I was in high school."

Melissa nodded remembering how horrible that time had been for Blake. She was worried about him constantly. Then his mom changed her mind and moved back home.

Blake swallowed hard. "He told me at the hospital that he blamed me for all the problems. In his twisted way of thinking back then, he wanted to hurt me because he was totally alone after mom passed. He couldn't bring mom back to life and he couldn't force me to do anything because of the military. When I came home he was on parole for another drug charge. I asked if he'd seen you and that I needed to find you. He got furious."

Confused, she asked, "Why would he be upset that you asked about me?"

"He didn't want me to be happy. He was hurt and wanted to hurt me." Blake looked down and released a deep breath. "The only way he knew how to really hurt me was to threaten you."

Melissa's back straightened up and she adjusted herself on his lap. "What do you mean?"

He looked back up at her. "He was a drunk and crazy man. He wanted nothing more than to control me and my mom. When mom died, he was left to face himself alone and didn't like what he saw. So, to get back at me for taking the control away from him, he told me he'd come after you. He said that if I ever told anyone about what he'd done to me or my mom that he'd hurt you. If I thought that it was ok to take everything away from him, then he would take what was precious to me. He knew that was you. He knew your schedule and told me he would keep tabs on what you were doing." He paused. "I did what I thought was best to help my mom but he found her anyway and forced her to move back. And we both know what happened to her after she was back there. I knew I had to be smarter when it came to you."

Melissa silently nodded.

"When that weekend was over and I never got to see you, especially after my dad's threats, I figured I'd missed my chance to change your mind. So, I didn't try to contact you again. I didn't want you to be connected with me in case dad decided to act on his threats.

Every so often I would try to look you up and see what you were up to but never had any luck."

"Blake, I had no idea." She remembered being both relieved and heartbroken that he came by. "It was hard for me to find out that you'd come to the house and been so close. I couldn't stand the thought that you might want nothing to do with me. I didn't want to see you hurt. But in doing so, I hurt you more than I ever wanted to."

"I'm not going to say I understand because I don't. I wish you'd have given me the chance to make my own choice. I thought you knew me better than that." His pain evident in his voice.

"I was wrong, Blake. I was afraid. I had no idea what I was going to do and I kept thinking that you didn't deserve that. You deserved to be happy and chase after all those big dreams you talked about." She wiped the tears from her eyes and dropped them to his chest. "It was selfish of me to hide from you. I didn't want to face the possibility that you'd reject me. If I could go back, I would handle it differently."

"I only wanted those dreams as long as you were with me. We both made mistakes and would change things if we could." His hands relaxed the firm hold he had around her. "I didn't meet Jennifer until 3 years later."

Melissa looked back up at him, anxious to hear where this was going.

"I was miserable and felt like my whole world was empty without you. All the guys around me kept ragging on me about hooking up with all the girls we saw. They didn't understand why I was so stuck on someone who didn't want me." Melissa flinched at his words. He squeezed her hand. "I decided I needed to move on but it wasn't the same. Jennifer deserved to be loved passionately and without any reservation just like every woman. I thought I could give her that. But in some way, I think we both knew I couldn't. She craved that kind of love and I couldn't give it to her. That's probably the reason she cheated on me."

He looked deep into her eyes and she felt like she could see everything behind them. He cupped her cheek with one hand. "You're it for me, Melissa. I first fell in love with you at seventeen. I didn't think I could possibly love you more than I did standing in the sunflowers with you. But I do. The way I felt about you back then doesn't hold a candle to how much I love you now." She closed her eyes and more tears fell on his thumbs. "Melissa."

She looked up at him.

"I'm so glad you have Wyatt. I'm glad that God gave you a beautiful miracle through such a horrible nightmare." He kissed her forehead, her right cheek, and her left cheek. He pulled back and her favorite ocean blue eyes looked deep into her own. "I love you, Melissa, in spite of the secrets, the pain, and the time lost. I don't want to be apart from you ever again."

The words she never thought he'd say to her, he said them and even more words than she could've imagined. All the fear, doubt, worry, and longing she'd been prisoner to for so many years evaporated like rain puddles in the Texas heat. She could see the possibility of peace, happiness, and love.

Blake wrapped his arms around her and pulled her tight to him. She returned his embrace and allowed herself to fall completely.

Chapter 26

Melissa paused washing dishes when she noticed Gram watching her from the doorway of the kitchen. "You know I noticed Blake's truck is parked in the driveway. He may want some company."

Melissa hadn't talked to Gram about what happened with Blake two days ago. She felt like she was a teenager again. They had been texting nonstop. Blake was busy clearing all his dad's debts.

"You know I've made two cherry pies. We only need one. Why don't you take the other over to Blake's?" Gram smiled.

Melissa finished drying the last pan and set it aside. "I've got to get Wyatt to bed. Maybe I'll take it tomorrow."

"Wyatt's already in his room reading and may even fall asleep soon." She picked up the pie and held it out to Melissa. "Please, it's from me."

"Ok. I'll take him the pie." She did want to see him. She paused before turning for the door. "Are you ok?"

"Yes, dear. You go spend some time with Blake." She turned and headed down the hall.

Stepping out into the warm summer night, Melissa noticed the front room light was still on across the street. Blake opened the door after the first knock. He was dressed only in gym shorts leaving his bare chest exposed. The corners of his mouth curved up when he saw it was her. "Hey."

"Hey," she smiled back trying to keep her eyes from wandering down his body. "I brought you a pie. Gram made two and insisted you have one."

"Thanks," He took it from her and stepped back allowing her to enter. "I've missed you." He leaned in and kissed her cheek.

"I've missed you too."

Blake closed the door behind her and went to place the pie on kitchen counter. She took a seat on the sofa and slipped out of her sandals. There was a baseball game on the TV. He came around the sofa and plopped down next to her.

"How's Wyatt doing?" he asked.

She shifted in her seat to get a better look at him. "He's good, missing baseball games. We've been able to do a lot more together now that tutoring is over."

"That's good. When do you have to go back to school?" He raised his arm across the back of the sofa. When his hand lightly brushed her shoulder, goosebumps ran down her arms from his touch. He smiled and she knew he was pleased with the effect he had on her.

She straightened her back and remembered he asked her a question. "I've got a few more weeks. Then the kids show up the week after that."

"Hard to believe summer's almost over." Blake took a drink of his water bottle and returned it to the coffee table.

"I know. Oh, I wanted to ask you how everything went with your dad's estate?"

"Good. I've got everything straightened out I think." He tugged her closer to him.

She wanted to ask him more but the sound of cheers caused Blake to look up at the TV. Of course, a baseball game was on. Melissa took that time to sneak a peek at Blake. It had been a long time since she had seen him without a shirt on making it a struggle to stay at eye level. His shoulders were broad and the lines dipped as they connected to his biceps. His chest had filled out and his stomach looked like the washboard Gram had next to the fireplace. Gone was the lean long legged kid she first fell in love with. He was strong, confident, and oh so handsome. Ok, he was hot. Her sexual desires hadn't been this enticed in years. He took a drink of his water bottle and it snapped Melissa back from her trance.

She hadn't felt tempted to be physical with a guy in years. Though she never acted on it, she couldn't pretend those feelings weren't there. After the rape, she didn't want to be close to any man. But being next to Blake, she felt herself wanting nothing but that.

They sat silent for a little bit and watched the baseball game. "Do you mind if I use your restroom really quick?" She stood and tugged at her shirt.

"Sure." He stayed seated but she could feel him watch her walk down the hall.

She gripped the counter and stared into the mirror. So much had happened in the past two months and she was so happy about it. Now she was here in his house alone and she couldn't deny the draw to him. It was like he was her perfect drug and she couldn't keep her mind g-rated. She ran her fingers through her hair and sighed. She wasn't dressed up fancy, just a simple halter top and jean shorts. She shook her head. "Get a grip. You're not a teenage girl anymore," she said to her reflection. Taking one last look in the mirror, she stepped back into the hall. When she entered the living room again it was empty. She looked around and called out to Blake.

"I'm in the kitchen," he answered.

She walked through the kitchen door and saw him at the sink. The muscles in his back were flexing as he washed a plate. Noticing her standing there, he held out a water bottle. "Are you thirsty?"

"Thank you," she said taking the bottle. She leaned up against the counter next to him and took a long swig of the water. He dried his hands and then turned toward her. She blew out a slow breath. *Eyes up. Eyes up.*

Blake took a side step in front of her and laid the towel down on the counter behind her. She felt her pulse increase at how close Blake was to her. Their chests were only inches from touching. As if he felt the same thing he paused. His eyes drifted down her and then back up with a smile spreading across his face. He took a step toward her. "You look beautiful." He leaned down and kissed her bare shoulder exposed by her halter top. "I love this shirt."

Blake never shied away from giving compliments and it made her heart flutter to think that she looked good to him. He backed away leaving Melissa pressed against the counter. She closed her eyes trying to catch her breath. His hand ran down her arm, lacing his fingers with hers. Then he lead her back into the living room. She settled next to him and allowed herself to fall into his side. She laid her head on his shoulder.

"Are you tired?" he asked.

"No, just enjoying the company." She looked up at him.

As if frozen in place they simply stared at each other, both seeming to fight the temptation. Blake gave way first, slowly leaning in and he pressed his lips to hers. She didn't flinch or shy away from his touch. In fact, she craved it. He pulled her close deepening the kiss, igniting a passion between them. His hands slowly slipped into her hair, the tips of his fingers gripping her neck. His touch set her skin on fire and she couldn't get enough. She slowly ran her hands over his bare shoulders stopping on his biceps. It felt so good. There was no worry about being physical with Blake.

Blake's resolve gave a little more and his kisses became hungry. She became bolder and slid one leg over his legs to straddle his lap. Suddenly, she felt his body tense and Blake slammed on the brakes. He kissed her one more time and pushed her back so he could look at her face. "Melissa, we can't."

"Just a little longer. We'll stop I promise. I finally feel comfortable being this way. Please, I've missed you." She leaned in and kissed him again. His hands settled on her thighs landing dangerously close to the hem of her skirt. A moan escaped his throat and it made Melissa's confidence sore. He felt as good as she did. But once again he pushed her back.

"I've missed you too. I'm a guy in love with you and I can't guarantee that I'll always be able to stop." He took a deep breath. "I promised."

Her heart fell to her feet. She had wanted so bad to feel close to him to let him know she loved him and he stopped it. They were still close enough that she could feel his raspy breath on her face. "I promised too but...," she dropped her head. "I finally have someone I trust enough to be this intimate with. I want to be close to you. I'll stop." He tilted his head back and looked at the ceiling. She felt her chest start to cave. "Do you not want to be with me?"

His head snapped forward. "Yes. I can't begin to tell you how bad. Melissa, you mean more to me than that. I want to be that guy you feel comfortable with. The guy that makes you forget about what that jack—" Melissa flinched at the thought of her rapist. The rise and fall in his chest slowed. "I'm sorry. I want to treat you like the treasure you are. I can't let my guard down. I want to save that for us when it's right." He kissed her forehead before gently moving her off his lap back onto the couch. He got up and grabbed a t-shirt from the back of the recliner.

She stood quickly, embarrassed that she even thought about doing something like this. She never intended for it to get to that point. It wasn't who she was but somehow she wanted it with Blake. The fear and pain had disappeared with him and she loved the way it made her feel. She walked over to the front door needing to get control of herself.

Blake sighed. "Melissa, it's not that I don't *want* you. I made a promise to the girl of my dreams when I was eighteen and I've kept it so far." She heard him take a step toward her. "I don't want you to do something that you'll regret later. And I know for a fact I would because I would get carried away. I'm not going to put you through that."

The sincerity in his tone didn't lift her spirits. He was right. Melissa pressed her eyes tightly together. It had been so long since she wanted to feel close to someone, to be wanted by someone. She heard Blake take a few steps in her direction and her body tensed. He must have seen it because he stopped.

"Mel, I—"

She straightened her back. "Blake, I would've stopped. I didn't think that's where tonight was going. I just want... I just thought... I-I'm going to go." She started to open the door when Blake's hand pushed it back shut. She dropped her head and felt the tears burn the back of her eyes.

"I can't let you leave with us like this." He nudged her shoulders to turn her around but she refused. She couldn't look at him.

"I'm embarrassed and just want to be alone." She reached for the door knob again and he grabbed her hand. "Blake, please. Let's talk about this tomorrow. We—"

"I'm not going to be here tomorrow."

Everything inside her stopped, like all time ceased to exist. She pulled her hand away. She knew in that instance that he was leaving. Is that why he pushed her off his lap? Had he decided to take the job in North Carolina?

The silence between them was deafening. She couldn't bring herself to look at him. She finally felt like she had pushed the fear and doubt away but it started to rear its ugly head again. If only he would wrap his arms around her and cast out the fear that racked her body but he didn't move. He stood a few feet away silent.

"You're leaving?"

He nodded and answered, "Yes, I have to go back to North Carolina. My house is there and—"

Melissa stopped listening and felt a sudden urge to flee. "I can't do this, Blake." She opened the door to leave but he reached over her shoulder and slammed it shut with more force than before.

"Melissa, just listen to me! It's not what you think—"

"You made me fall in love with you again and now you're leaving! That's what I think!"

He took her hands in his again and pleaded, "Don't do this. Why do you assume the worst in me? You're not even giving me a chance to tell you why I'm going!"

She quickly pulled her hands away. "Maybe I assume the worst because I've seen the worst."

"But I'm not him, Melissa!" He fell back on his heals. "I'm not him," he said breathlessly.

Panic swelled in her chest. Blake's hurt and frustration was evident across his face. "I never said you were."

"You didn't have to." Blake shook his head in disgust. "You're too wrapped up in your own fear that you can't see that you keep hurting me, or maybe you don't really care."

She gasped at the fact that he could think that. All the decisions she ever made, she did with him in mind.

He scoffed at her response. "You don't think so? Gosh, Mel, I have pursued you when you gave me no reason to. I did my best to build a relationship with Wyatt without knowing about his father. I pushed aside my frustration and gave you time to tell me what happened. A few days ago, I told you that I wanted a life with you. Your rape doesn't define you and that's not how I see you. I've been trying to show you how much I love you but you always doubt me. It doesn't ever seem like what I say or do is enough. I don't think I'll ever be enough for you and honestly..." He ran his hands through his hair. "I'm not sure I can keep trying to be."

Melissa felt everything inside her stop. She bit the inside of her lip in an attempt to keep her tears from falling. His words pierced her heart. "I guess that's my answer."

After shutting the door, she quickly ran home without looking back. Once inside the safety of her house, she pressed her back against the door, slid down to the ground, and pulled her legs to her chest. The realization that the second chance she had with Blake had come to an end came crashing in like a tidal wave. Her whole body wrenched and the tears poured down her cheeks.

Everything Melissa thought she was ready to share with Blake had suddenly been stripped away in less than an hour. She finally thought she was ready to give her whole heart to Blake again. Blake's words rang in her head.

I don't think I'll ever be enough for you and honestly I'm not sure I can keep trying to be.

Melissa couldn't believe he thought that. He was everything she'd ever wanted. He was the only man she'd ever loved.

How could she be so stupid to allow herself to live in fear? She hurt him all over again. She did doubt and question everything, especially him. She wanted to love Blake. She *did* love him, there was no question. He'd come back for her eight years ago. He had pursued her the past two months. He accepted and loved her when he found out everything about her rape. He was honest and loving. He was her happily ever after and her best friend. But now she was afraid she'd lost him forever.

Chapter 27

Melissa grabbed two glasses of tea and a water bottle then headed to the back porch. Gram was gliding in her rocking chair looking out at the sunflower field. Placing the bottle and one glass on the table next to Gram, Melissa took a seat on the swing.

"Where's that little boy of yours?" Gram asked.

"He's helping mom bake cookies for the bake sale at church." Melissa took a big swig of her tea.

"Oh good. How have you been, dear?"

Melissa looked over at her. "I'm good. I've had to start my preparations for school since we're so close to my check in day. I did my last column for the paper this past week. It's time to get ready for school to start and I can't give as much time to the paper as I'd like. But it's good we're about to get back into a regular schedule."

This summer had thrown her plenty of curve balls mostly because of Blake. It had been almost a week since she had seen him. His drive way was empty which meant he was in North Carolina. Any time he came to mind her stomach churned thinking of the loss.

"Melissa?"

"Hmm?" Melissa raised her eyes brows at Gram.

"I've done my best to stay away from the elephant in the room but I would like to talk to you about it if you're willing."

Melissa dropped her eyes to the glass in her hands. Gram had stayed away from the topic weighing heavy on Melissa's heart and she was appreciative of that. She hadn't talked to anyone about Blake in hopes that it would make it easier to move on but it didn't work for her eight years ago. Why would it now? Gram was probably right. "Ok."

"Melissa."

She swallowed hard and looked up to see Gram's sympathetic eyes.

"You know I love you and more than anything I want you to find happiness. I want you and Wyatt to both be happy. I don't want the two of you living life with a missing piece to your family."

"You and mom are our family, Gram."

Gram smiled. "It has been such a joy to see you brought back to life these past few months. But dear, the last week has been the complete opposite. You're distant and lonely."

Melissa knew what Gram meant. She'd been quiet and hadn't gone out hardly at all. She'd thrown herself into getting ready for school to start. Jade even asked her to go out and she declined.

"I desperately want you to talk to me about it, about Blake."

Speaking out loud about her feelings was going to make it all so real. True. Final. "I don't know what to think, Gram. I thought that I was ready to be with someone, but I don't know."

"My opinion is that you *are* ready."

"I hoped that I would be someday."

"What's wrong with Blake?" Gram asked.

She hesitated not sure she wanted to reveal what had happened between them. She was embarrassed and felt like the hole she was trying to heal was being torn open again.

"Melissa, I don't know what happened between you two but I know that you both care deeply for each other. I believe Blake enjoys Wyatt as well. Surly whatever has happened can be fixed."

But it can't be fixed. Melissa pressed her lips together. "I don't think so, Gram."

"And why not?"

"It's my fault. I pushed him away again." She looked out at the big blue Texas sky. "He said I believe the worst in him."

After a moment Gram asked, "Do you?"

"I didn't want to. He said..." She caught the emotion in her throat. "He said he doesn't feel like he'll ever be enough for me and he's not sure he can keep trying to be." She felt one tear break through and she swiped it away.

"So, Blake feels like you believe the worst in him and no matter what he does to try and show you he cares you can't accept it?"

Melissa felt her chest tighten. She didn't want to doubt Blake. He'd given her no reason to think that. "I told you I don't want to. He's the only person I've ever loved." She wiped away another loose tear. "And now he's left and gone back to North Carolina."

Gram was quiet for several heartbeats. "I had noticed his driveway was empty."

Melissa took a deep breath. "The night I took him the extra pie we had a fight. We sat and talked for a little bit. I just wanted to be close to him." Embarrassment flushed her cheeks. She looked at Gram and it was obvious Gram was more perceptive than Melissa thought. "Nothing happened. I would've stopped but he stopped first and I let it hurt my feelings. In return, I just wanted to be alone. But he wouldn't let me leave because he said he was going back to North Carolina." Melissa felt the moisture returning to her eyes as she thought about standing in his living room after he pushed her away. Even if his motives were noble and she agreed with him, it still didn't change the fact that she felt rejected.

"Do you know how long he'll be gone?"

"No."

"Do you know why he needed to leave?"

"Something about his house."

"So you don't really know." Melissa looked over at Gram and she slowed her rocker to a stop. "How did you know he was leaving?"

"He said so." Hurt was replacing the anger in her voice.

"Has he tried to contact you?"

Melissa sighed and said, "He's called me once the day after he left."

"And you didn't answer it?"

She sighed. "I was helping Wyatt in the backyard and left my phone inside."

"Why not call him back?"

She looked down. "I don't know."

"I hate to see you mad at him. That boy has always chased after you. I remember him asking everyone about you when he came back to town when you were pregnant. Even now as adults, he cares more than I think you know. Maybe he was going to tell you why and you didn't let him tell you."

The question hit her square in the chest. "I don't want to be with someone who might leave for something better." Her voice started to shake and the tears overpowered her eyelids. "Dad left us for something better. A nameless boy stole what was special about me and left me without a second look. I must not be worth much if that's how they see me."

Gram stood and pulled Melissa up from the swing. Placing her wrinkled hand on Melissa's wet cheek. "Oh, Melissa."

She fell into Gram's arms and released it all. She sank into Gram's chest. The bitterness, anger, and hurt escaped as she cried. Everything she kept hidden deep inside, what she believed about herself, had become facts in her mind. As her tears slowed, she looked up at Gram to see there were tears in her eyes as well.

"My sweet, Melissa. I can't answer for why hurtful things happen in our lives. I can't answer for why your dad left you and your mom. I don't know what was going on in the mind of the boy who raped you. I don't know why Blake is having to leave right now. You cannot believe those horrible things. They happened to you but they don't define you." Gram brushed a loose piece of hair away from Melissa's face. "You can't hold that anger and bitterness in your heart. It will consume everything in you and keep you from the blessings God has set aside for you."

After a moment, Gram turned them both toward the sunflower field. "Do you know why sunflowers are my favorite flower?"

Melissa shook her head no as she wiped her face.

"Sunflowers need constant light. They accomplish this by turning their heads to follow the sun as it moves across the sky. They seek out the light and follow it wherever it goes." She paused taking in the giant faces to the north of the house. Melissa could see how much Gram loved them. Her eyes were bright and smile soft. "Helen Keller once said, 'Keep your face to the sunshine and you cannot see the shadows. It's what the sunflowers do.' I just love that." She smiled at Melissa. "You have to flee from the darkness in your life. Be like a sunflower."

Melissa smiled and looked back out over the field. "I didn't know that about sunflowers."

"It's the perfect example of how we should fight bitterness, not letting it take root in our heart." Gram paused. "It's like there are broken pieces of glass from all the hurt and pain in life at your feet. It's one thing to try not to step on the glass and accidently get stuck here and there. But it's another to pick them up and clench them in your hand."

Gram took Melissa's hand in her own. "Those broken relationships and memories have to be mourned and released into God's hands. That burden can easily turn into bitterness if you don't allow yourself to let it go and love."

"I thought I had..." Melissa's voice trailed off.

"I believe that you *are* ready to fall in love. I believe you have and quite possibly never stopped loving. I just pray you are able to release the fear of being abandoned. Maybe then you can experience the kind of love God intends for you." Gram cupped the side of Melissa's face. "Blake definitely chases after what's on his heart. I know it's true that he has always loved you and that he still does. It's all over that boy's face. I don't want you to believe he doesn't."

Melissa wanted to believe that. "What if he doesn't come back?"

Gram took Melissa's hand in her own and squeezed. "Perhaps it's your turn to chase after him."

Melissa nodded letting Gram know that she heard her. Melissa walked back into the house with the truth of Gram's words taking root in her heart. She stood in Gram's front window and looked across the street at Blake's empty house. She wished she had released the pain a long time ago. She wanted to love and be loved in the most beautiful way and she knew who she wanted that to be with.

When she was seventeen all Melissa had ever wanted was to love Blake. Now she found herself wanting nothing more than to combine her love for him with her love for Wyatt. Together they could create a beautiful family. He had been honorable to her and she let her longing for love hurt her.

She hadn't given him the chance to tell her why he was leaving and to explain. She hadn't listened.

I'm not him, Melissa! She could see the desperation in Blake's face when he said those words.

She was carrying the pain of rejection from her father and the belief that she was worthless from her rape into their relationship. She was making Blake pay for something he never did to her. Even with all the horrible and wonderful things she'd lived through, Blake never made her feel like he held that against her. He had listened to her talk about her rape and loved that she had Wyatt. He never let a moment pass that she didn't feel valued when he was with her.

She didn't know when he'd be back. One thing was clear, no matter how long she had to wait she wouldn't let Blake go without telling him how she truly felt. She didn't want to look at her future and him not be in it.

Chapter 28

Blake took his coffee mug from the barista and swallowed a big drink. That's just what he needed after his long seventeen-hour drive. It may be dinner time but he didn't care, he needed coffee. He squeezed through the crowd on his way out the door and bumped into James.

"Oh, sorry man." Blake brushed the spilled drink off his hand.

James brushed his shirt and laughed. "Not a problem. It's crazy in there, huh?"

"Just like any other day." Blake noticed James was sporting a nice tan. "How was your honeymoon?"

James' smile spread ear to ear. "It was amazing! Mexico is beautiful and we had the best time. One week isn't near long enough."

"I bet." Blake hoped to have what James had one day.

"I'm really sorry we weren't here for your dad's memorial," James said sympathetically.

Blake slumped slightly at the reminder. "Oh, don't worry about it. I'm glad that he isn't having to battle cancer anymore."

James nodded. "I hear you've been gone for a week or so. Is everything ok?"

"Yeah. I had to go back to North Carolina to close on my house."

"Wait, you're moving back?" James asked.

Shaking his head Blake said, "No. I sold my house. The one I bought when Jennifer and I were together. I had to clean up some loose ends out there and it took longer than I expected."

"So, where are you going to live?"

"Well I've been offered a job at the V.A. hospital here in Dallas and I still have my dad's house. I haven't decided if I'm going to sell it and move closer to the hospital or not."

"That's great man! I'm sure if you sell his house you have your reasons but if you don't mind me saying, there's a girl across the street that might be a good reason to keep it."

Blake wasn't so sure. James simply smiled and slapped Blake's back then turned toward the cafe door. Before entering he looked back and said, "Hey, Blake."

Blake raised his eye brows at him.

"Remember, love looks good on you." With a smile, James disappeared behind the glass door.

Blake got in his truck and pulled out on the road, headed home to rest. He hadn't stopped thinking about Melissa since she left his house a week ago. He relived that night over and over in his head. He never meant to hurt her feelings and it took everything in him to push her off his lap. Since they were teenagers he'd wanted nothing more than to be with her in that way. But no matter how bad either of them wanted it, he knew he made the right choice.

The day after he left he tried to call her. She didn't answer or return his call. Perhaps she needed space and he figured what needed to be said shouldn't be done over the phone anyway. He didn't know what to expect the next time he saw her. He had gotten mad and said things he didn't mean. He had been in love with Melissa since he was seventeen. He knew he couldn't just shut off his feelings for her.

Pushing open the door to his house, Blake dropped his bags just inside. He saw that Melissa's car wasn't in the drive at Gram's. It would be best to wait for her to return home before going over. He was worried that he may have caused a bigger problem than he intended. What if she didn't want to talk to him? What if she shut him out of her life again? He felt pressure building in his chest. He looked up at the sky and saw that he had a few more hours before sunset.

There was only one place that could help him gain clarity before he talked with Melissa. He turned and crossed over the yellow threshold.

******

Melissa finished putting the leftovers from dinner in the fridge. It was nice to have a night in, while her mom, Julie, took her car and went out with her book club. She turned off the kitchen lights and ventured into the living room. Her mom was reading in the corner and Gram had gone off to bed. She turned and headed down the hall to Wyatt's room where he was fast asleep. She brushed her hand over his hair and smiled. She loved how peaceful he looked when he slept. She tucked the blanket tight around him and turned off his bedside lamp. Before heading to bed she wanted to get a glass of water. When she reached the bottom of the stairs, she paused by Gram's front window. Her heart skipped when she saw the very thing she had been waiting for. Blake's truck was parked in the driveway.

When Blake first left Shaw Creek a week ago, Melissa wasn't sure she would be able to talk to him again. The embarrassment and hurt was more than she could handle. Then she was scared he'd finally made up his mind to move on. As the days went by, her heart softened and she was worried she'd lost him forever. She desperately wanted to talk to him. Gram's words had taken root in her heart and Melissa knew she couldn't let her pride stand in the way of a relationship with Blake.

She slipped on her sandals and ran across the street. After knocking on his door a few times, she realized he wasn't there. Stepping back out in his driveway she looked down the street in case he went for a run. Nothing. Then she looked toward the sunflowers. Maybe he was out there. Trying to stay quiet, Melissa pushed through the sunflowers and paused before stepping out into the clearing. There sitting at the bottom of the old oak tree was the man she wanted to see. She walked slowly around the opposite side of the tree and saw that

Blake's eyes were closed with his head leaning against the trunk. Careful not to touch him she took her place next to him. She figured he had heard her as he straightened his back against the tree slightly. She was sad when he didn't take her hand like he used to.

When he didn't move more, she realized it was going to take everything in her to do this. She had to lay everything on the line. It was her turn to pursue *him*. She pushed up off the tree and knelt down in front of him. His face looked sad, nervous perhaps. Mustering up all her courage she spoke. "Blake?"

His chest rose and fell. A single tear ran down his cheek and it took everything in Melissa for her to not touch him. Then slowly his eyes opened and met hers. They were the deepest blue she'd ever seen.

"Melissa." She barley heard him.

"I've been wanting to talk to you all week." His eyes were locked on hers so she continued. "There's so much I need to apologize for. You've always been a best friend to me and I have been the worst possible friend to you. I never meant to push you or make you struggle with your convictions. And I'm thankful that you stuck to yours."

She dropped her eyes for a second and braced herself to admit what she hadn't been able to before. "I've been abandoned by my dad and had everything innocent stripped from me by a stranger. They both left me without looking back. When you told me that you were leaving I went blank. I didn't even want to know why. Which is crazy now that I think about it. But at the time all I could think was that you were choosing to leave me too."

"Mel—" Blake began to speak.

"No, Blake. I need to finish, please." He nodded and she took another deep breath. "You have been nothing but supportive and caring to me, even after I abandoned you. You never gave me a reason to believe you'd do what others had. I never meant for you to ever feel like you weren't enough for me. You are more than enough. I was just afraid I wouldn't be for you. I shouldn't have pulled away from you the way that I did and left without giving you a chance to explain. I'm sorry." She remained still bracing for his response.

Blake released a deep breath and then spoke. "I need to apologize to you too." When he slid his hands under hers and gripped them tight, hope lit inside her heart for the first time in nearly a week. "I never meant to make you feel like I was pushing you away. I could see it in your eyes and the way you stood there closed off from me. I can imagine how hard it is to be intimate with anyone after what you went through. I'm sorry." He brought her fingers to his face and lightly kissed them.

Melissa knew there was more she had to say. She squeezed his hand tight. "When you told me that you loved me that last time, I couldn't bring myself to say it back. Not because of you but because of my own fear. I was scared to be vulnerable again because of what you might see if you really looked at me. I didn't let myself fall for anyone or get close enough to even picture myself falling in love again. Then I ran into you, the last person I ever expected to see again. When I did your interview and it forced me to face you, I saw you in a different light and my fears seemed to fade away. For the first time in years, my heart thought it was possible to love and be loved again."

Blake hadn't moved or released her hands and Melissa rubbed her thumb over them. "I finally got to the place where I knew I wanted to love again, more than I ever had before. The problem is that I was holding too tight to what I thought I'd become because of my past. I let that one horrible thing distort my view of all the beautiful things in my life. I want to love again, really love someone with everything I am." She felt the tears break free, finding their way down her cheeks. "The truth is I don't think I ever stopped loving you either, Blake."

Blake's eyes filled with tears. Now it was time to say what she had been too afraid to say before. It meant she would be taking the last step she needed to take in order to move on with faith and trust that the future would be better than anything in her past. "I never imagined I would get a second chance at love with you, but here you are. I'm so glad you came back into my life. You broke through my walls and wanted me in spite of what was in my past. You forgave me and accepted Wyatt as a part of my life." She placed her hand over his heart. "I loved you when we were kids and thought that pushing you away proved that. I was wrong. I didn't really know what love was. You've shown me what true love is. It is kind, patient, passionate, forgiving, never ending, and all consuming. Thank you for not giving up on me." She took a deep breath. "I, Melissa Adair, love you Blake Knoll. I love you. I don't want you to just hope for it. I want you to know it. I want you to believe it because I do. I love you."

A smile curled up Blake's cheeks. He cupped one side of her face and pulled her close until his lips found hers. Her heart soared at his touch and the weight she had been carrying lifted with it. Pressing his forehead against hers he whispered, "Melissa, my Melissa."

Leaning back to see her face, Blake wiped the tears away. "I've said this recently but I will say it again, and keep saying it all day every day if I have to. I love you, Melissa. I love all of you. I love your son. I love your journey back to me. You've always been the one for me. I could never love anyone the way that I love you."

This time it was Melissa who pulled him in for a kiss. All the pain from the past and the fear of the future disappeared as she completely let the strength and love Blake was pouring into their kiss surround her. She slowly released him and slid back into her spot beside him curling up under his arm. The sky was lit in the most beautiful mix of oranges and pinks. Melissa's eyes soaked the colors in as they danced off the pond. The sunflowers rustled in the cool breeze. She never wanted this moment to end. There was one question that she still wanted to ask. "Can I ask you a question?"

"Anything."

"Why did you leave and go back to North Carolina?"

He shifted to look at her next to him then kissed her forehead. "You remember me telling you I bought a house for when I wanted to settle down?"

"Yeah." Like she could forget.

"Well, I hadn't decided what I was going to do once dad passed away. It was always an option to go back and work things out there. I didn't know if I had a reason to stay back here in Texas. I had several people who were willing to help me get a job. Like my sergeant telling me about that veteran assistant job so I did a phone interview. They told me I'd be crazy not to come back."

Melissa could understand why they told him that.

"But after the 4th of July I knew I wanted to be here. You're my reason to be here, you and Wyatt. So, I put it up for sale and luckily it sold in a few weeks. It just took me longer to settle everything out there than I hoped."

"You really want to be here with us?" she asked.

"I do." Blake nodded. "You see, there's this beautiful brown eyed girl who lived across the street from me and I knew I was going to spend the rest of my life with her. Now things didn't really go as I planned. She had someone hurt her in a way I can never understand. As a result, she lost who she was to the lies those things made her believe about herself. She forgot she was valuable, important, and deserving of love. She's a good friend and a great teacher. The best part is that she has an amazing son who adores her."

"Blake..." she whispered.

He smiled and shook his head. "I've got to tell you the rest." He kissed the tip of her nose. "She thought she could live her life alone just taking care of her son and I thought I could fall in love with someone else. We were both wrong. When I ran into her two months ago, I had a lot of questions. I had assumed that she found someone else and had been angry that she wouldn't talk to me. Can you believe that we were given the chance to become friends again? She wrote the most meaningful article about my life and I don't think I can tell her how much that meant to me. I realized I still loved her when I saw her with her son. She was laughing, at ease, and being goofy with him. She'd never been more beautiful to me. Then some other things happened good and bad. After it all, we finally exposed our demons and we realized it hadn't destroyed us. It felt like a dream, like we had finally got back to what I wanted all along. Now there was another fight and a short separation but you know what?"

"What?" she asked.

"I don't want to love her like I did when I was eighteen. I don't want to love her like I did when I saw her with her son on the 4th of July. I want to love her more than that, in a way that's hard to put into words but I'll try." He brought his hands around Melissa's face and smiled that knee weakening smile. "I want to love you like the moment I saw the blue sky after surviving my first sand storm: desperately, gratefully, passionately, and as if my whole life depends on it."

Blake pulled out a small black box from his pocket and Melissa gasped. "Blake…"

He leaned in just millimeters from their lips touching and said, "I love when you say my name." He kissed her and then pushed off the tree and got down on his knees in front of her. "There's one other thing I did when I was in North Carolina. I was planning on waiting a little bit but I don't think I can. I can't imagine my life without you. I spent eight years that way and I don't ever want to worry about that again." He popped open the box revealing a beautiful princess cut solitaire. "Melissa Jane Adair, will you marry me?"

With tears in her eyes she threw her arms around his neck and kissed him passionately.

"Is that a yes?" Blake asked laughing.

Melissa nodded. "Always."

Epilogue

One Year Later

Cami gave Melissa a side hug in accommodation for her growing mid-section. "I'm so happy for you, Melissa! This was the perfect place to have your wedding."

Melissa looked around the field. "Thank you. We couldn't imagine any other the place." She rubbed Cami's belly. "You are just glowing!"

"Oh thank you, even if you're lying. Being seven months pregnant in the dead of summer is something I wouldn't wish on my worst enemy." They both laughed.

"I'm so happy for you guys. You will be amazing parents."

Cami squeezed her arm. "I guess I better find James and get a dance or two in while my feet can withstand it. This baby definitely has the upper hand."

"Enjoy." Melissa watched her disappear amongst all the friends and family.

The sun was gorgeous providing the perfect lighting and the sunflowers just glowed like they each had a halo above their heads. Wyatt looked so good in his jeans, mint button down shirt, and silver vest, just like Blake. Blake was joking with him and some of the other family members. It warmed Melissa's heart to see the bond the two of them had developed over the past twelve months. Melissa smiled at Jade and Aly dancing their hearts out in the middle of everyone. Aly had moved in with Jade a few weeks ago and it was so good to be close again. They looked amazing out there with everyone. With the sunflowers providing the most amazing backdrop to the dance floor.

"The ceremony was absolutely stunning, Melissa." Gram wrapped her arms around Melissa in a hug only a grandmother could give. Melissa could see there were tears in her eyes. "This is the most beautiful wedding gown I've ever seen."

Melissa looked down at her gown. It wasn't anything fancy or near as elaborate as Cami's had been. It was a simple laced tea length strapless white dress. "Thank you, Gram." Melissa kissed her cheek.

"It could also be the bride inside the dress. True love is a beautiful thing." Gram patted her arm. "I'm going to get something to drink."

Melissa watched her walk over and sighed at the feeling of love that was evident in everyone there. She turned and walked toward the ceremony arch located at the base of the old oak tree. The candle lit lanterns hung from the different branches with accents of crystals which reflected the light throughout the space. She walked under the arch and around the large trunk. Her fingers ran across the bark of the tree and she paused when she found the worn-down spots on the opposite side. She smiled to herself thinking of what this place meant to her and Blake. She stepped away and stopped at the edge of the pond. The feel of the cool grass on her bare feet made her smile.

The sun had set and the soft light danced across the pond. Looking down at her dress she ran her fingers across the delicate laced body. She felt beautiful. She was in love and had a wonderful son, family, and friends that supported her. She felt like a priceless treasure that the man of her dreams never wanted to let go. All the things she'd wanted in life had finally come true.

Looking up at the clear starry sky, Melissa was at peace. *Thank you, Lord, for all the blessings you've given me. I know I don't deserve them but I'm thankful. I'm so happy with Blake. He and Wyatt have bonded better than in my wildest dreams. I love that he can be a father to Wyatt. I love the way Blake loves him regardless of him not being his own. Thank you.*

She turned and saw Blake laughing with some friends next to the dance floor. She smiled to herself before turning back to look at the sky over the pond.

God, I know I made mistakes. I'm thankful for forgiveness, yours and Blake's. I'm thankful for second chances. I didn't know I could love someone this much. I pray that I never take for granted getting to be with my first and only love. And to think it can be greater than anything I've ever felt before.

Melissa wrapped her arms around her waist taking in the beautiful Texas night. After a few moments, she felt her favorite pair of strong hands slide across her arms and pull her close to him from behind.

"Have I told you how beautiful you look tonight?" Blake's whisper tickled her neck. He kissed her bare shoulder and she leaned her head into his.

"Oh, once or twice." She couldn't help but smile.

They stood holding each other for a minute looking out at the pond before Blake turned her around to face him. She slid her hands up his chest and settled around his neck. "You look mighty nice tonight yourself."

Looking down at his button down shirt and vest he shrugged. "I do try to be a little fancy every once in a while. If it's for you then I'll dress up any time." He winked.

A new song started playing and he spun her out then back in to him. Her face lit up with a smile and he came in close for a quick kiss. She rested her head on his chest allowing the beautiful melody to wrap around the two of them. This was home and she never wanted to leave his embrace.

After a minute, she looked back up to him. The different flakes of blue were more prominent in his eyes as the light sparkled off of them. His face was the happiest she had ever seen it. As they stared into each other's eyes, she noticed a rim of tears filling the bottom of Blake's eyes.

"What are you thinking?" she asked.

He tilted his head as he too searched her eyes. "I'm just thinking about how thankful I am for the life I have."

"How so?" she asked pleasantly and smiled in agreement with his answer.

"Oh, lots of things." He paused as he thought about it. "I'm thankful for the good and the bad things I've seen. I'm thankful for the lessons I learned. I'm thankful that God's plan for my life went beyond my home circumstance. It took me places I never dreamed I'd go. I learned so much about myself and what I'm capable of. I'm thankful for my time as a Marine."

She smiled and loved hearing him talk openly about it. "What else?"

Blake looked out toward the field and as they continued to glide with the music. "I'm thankful for Shasten Lane. I'm thankful for the sunflowers. I'm thankful for this old oak tree." He looked back at her. "When I was off across the world fighting a faceless enemy not knowing what lay ahead of me, do you know what helped me?"

"What?" Melissa asked.

"I would close my eyes and picture myself here. Sitting with you under a sky just like tonight. Holding your hand and listening to the peaceful song of the crickets. It's in those moments with you that I felt God's love most of all. I don't know how I would've made it through the darkest times if I didn't have you to escape out here with. Even though our paths took different turns I always held that close to me."

Melissa felt a tear run down her cheek and Blake softly wiped it away. "I'm thankful for your journey back to me and all that comes along with it. I'm thankful that you are the best mother to Wyatt. It is one of the most beautiful things to watch. I'm thankful that you let me be a part of his life. I love him more and more each day."

Melissa dropped her arms off his shoulders and wrapped them around his waist to match his hold of her. "Thank you for being a dad to him."

"I'm thank—"

"There's more?" Melissa interrupted.

"I'm almost done just a couple more things." He kissed her cheek. "I'm thankful you love writing in coffee shops and that you let me sit down with you that day." He kissed her other cheek. "I'm thankful for second chances." He kissed her lips softly then hovered over them. "I'm thankful for the ability to be with the only girl I've ever loved."

Blake slowed their sway to a stop and looked deeply in her eyes. Melissa's heart was full and she felt like she was in a dream. He leaned in and kissed her passionately. Once the kiss broke, they both had to catch their breath, their faces flushed.

"And I'm pretty excited about our honeymoon too!" Blake shot her a cheesy grin and Melissa couldn't help but laugh at him.

They had decided to honor their original promise to each other and wait until they were married. She was so glad they had.

"What about you?" Blake asked. "What are you thankful for?"

"Umm, I'm not sure how to follow that," Melissa teased.

He leaned in and gave her a quick kiss. "Try, babe."

"I would have to say that I'm thankful for everything you just said. I've been blessed beyond measure and I don't know that there are enough words to explain it."

Her voice caught as she thought over all the things that had led her to this point. She had faced abandonment, rejection, disrespect, and loneliness. She was guarded, defensive, and selfish. Yet she had come through on the other side and those things didn't hold refuge in her heart any more. It had been replaced with peace and gratitude. Releasing those things allowed her to remove the shards of glass stuck in her heart. Through God's grace a man came back into her life and broke through those walls. He didn't give up and helped carry her beyond the brokenness.

She cleared her throat. "If I had to name one thing that has been the biggest gift to me it would be that I get to love you. I get to love *you*, Mr. Knoll. I know that I am capable of great love, even after great pain." She placed her hand on Blake's face. "You, my sweet husband, deserve a chance at that great big beautiful love and I plan on being the one to love you that way."

"I'm going to do the same for you, Mrs. Knoll." Blake pulled her in for a sweet kiss. Melissa leaned her head against his chest and felt her heartbeat sync with his. They began to sway to the music again when the sunflowers caught her eye. Their giant faces glowed beneath the hanging lights. No matter what valleys were in her future, Melissa knew she wouldn't let the darkness grip her heart like it had in the past. She would keep those people full of hope, love, and light close, always searching for the sunflowers around her.

Please Leave a Review!

If you enjoyed this book you can leave a review on <u>Amazon</u> and <u>Goodreads</u> to help get the word out about Charity's book!

Continue the Series

To Believe in You – Colt & Aly

About the Author

Charity Christy writes contemporary clean romance designed to inspire, encourage, and tug at your heart strings. She believes the art of writing is one of the most powerful ways to share the power of forgiveness, the expanse of love, and the importance of your own story. Charity lives in Oklahoma with her husband, Brent, and their two boys. She received her Bachelor of Arts from Northeastern State University in Oklahoma. She loves blogging, traveling, photography, and genealogy. She finds the most enjoyment being outside, drinking hot tea, with a pen and paper, overlooking their family farm.

To get to know Charity more visit www.charitychristy.com. You can also find her on Facebook, Twitter, Instagram, and Pinterest.

Acknowledgements

First I want to thank my savior, Jesus Christ. I know that the creative passions that stir in my heart are from Him. I thank Him for setting my heart on fire for people and allowing my love for pen and paper to play a small part in hopefully helping others.

Brent – Thank you for telling me that I can do whatever my heart desires, for listening to me ramble on about the details bouncing around in my head, and taking care of the boys while I'm lost deep in thought. Your tender spirit encourages me when I feel doubt or less than. I could never repay you for the love you pour out on me daily. Thank you for taking this journey with me and here's to many more to come!

Mom & Dad – I'm not sure that I can say just what the two of you mean to me. I'm so thankful that you never discouraged my desire to write. You've always been my biggest cheerleaders and I know I couldn't have done any of this without your encouragement. It all started with me sitting around the kitchen table as a young girl telling you about my VERY detailed dreams and you listened to all of them. Now you've listened to me as I've written my first novel. I love you both more than I can say.

Rachel & Hannah – I have been blessed with some pretty amazing little sisters. I want to thank you for listening to me go on and on about this story. Thank you for the many Facetime chats and late night debates about where I wanted this story to go. Thank you for your honesty and excitement through this whole process.

WordGirls & COMPEL Small Group – I can never say thank you enough for what all you ladies have done for me the past year. I have learned so much about the writing process, publishing, and who I want to be as a writer from you all. Your prayers and accountability helped me keep faith at the forefront as I took this journey for the very first time. I can never repay you!

My LifeGroup – You are some of the most amazing people in my life. I'm so thankful for your spiritual encouragement, honest living, prayers, and friendships. I'm so glad that God brought you into my life and that we get to live this beautifully imperfect life together!

Jenny – You have been a huge help to me! I appreciate your encouragement and help in reading through my manuscript. You know how much I love grammar. Your time means the world to me. You're a great friend!

Nikki – Thank you so much for your honesty and willingness to help critique my manuscript. I appreciate you!

Crystal – I cannot begin to tell you how much I appreciate the time you took to listen to my rambling and help me through this process! You've become a great friend!

Candice – I cannot put into words what your help in editing my very first manuscript has meant to me. It's amazing to see what it was originally and what it is now! Your advice and encouragement was amazing and helped shape me into a much better writer. I owe you so much!

Victorine – Thank you so much for my beautiful cover! I absolutely love it!

www.ingramcontent.com/pod-product-compliance
Lightning Source LLC
Chambersburg PA
CBHW051458170626
46811CB00002B/540

* 9 7 8 0 6 9 2 8 9 6 0 4 4 *